HERE COMES JOHN

HERE COMES JOHN

short stories

BRIDGET O'CONNOR

JONATHAN CAPE
LONDON

First published 1993

1 3 5 7 9 10 8 6 4 2

© Bridget O'Connor 1993

First published in the United Kingdom in 1993 by
Jonathan Cape
Random House, 20 Vauxhall Bridge Road, London SW1V 2SA

These stories previously appeared in the following publications: 'Postcards' in *The
Picador Book of Contemporary Irish Fiction* (Picador, 1993); 'Here Comes John' in
Marxism Today; 'Ursula's Room' in *Cape 1*; 'Reader's Wife' in *Commonthread
Anthology* (Mandarin, 1989); 'Harp' in *Time Out*.

Random House Australia (Pty) Limited
20 Alfred Street, Milsons Point, Sydney,
New South Wales 2061, Australia

Random House New Zealand Limited
18 Poland Road, Glenfield,
Auckland 10, New Zealand

Random House South Africa (Pty) Limited
PO Box 337, Bergvlei, South Africa

Random House UK Limited Reg. No. 954009

A CIP catalogue record for this book
is available from the British Library

ISBN 0-224-03218-6

Typeset by Pure Tech Corporation, Pondicherry, India
Printed in Great Britain by
Mackays of Chatham PLC,
Chatham, Kent

CONTENTS

For Jim and Bridie O'Connor

KISSING TIME

SHE SAID, WHEN SHE COULD, 'How long have I got?'
The dentist's assistant wheeled away disgusted. The dentist
was young. He had alopecia (now that wasn't fair, was it?),
head like a kid's fight, the damage combed over, his fingers
in latex, the smell of new dollies. A hosepipe, the smell of
something a long, long time rotting. She lay back, cried . . .
The noise was tremendous: spluttering scraping, needles.
Needles of light. The dentist was yelling, 'Quite frankly,
young lady, never never never in my life . . . '

The dentist yelled, 'What did I tell you, I told you, use
short vibratory movements . . . the surfaces . . . not always
possible . . . clean between, up and down, *not* slash . . .
Floss . . . '

Seven feet of floss across the bathroom floor, in the bin,
floss webs. On the sink, teeth paraphernalia: dental gum,
interdental gum picks, angled toothbrushes. Anti-plaque
gargle gargle gag. Too much, too bloody late. Blood in the
toothpaste, rinse, gag, soft gums. Blood on the skin of an
apple.

Oh God, her teeth. She was going to lose her teeth.

With a tan they'd flash across 400 yards. In winter packed
and beige –

She smoked, they were purple behind (the dentist said, 'Oh for Christ sakes look! *Look!*'), like curd in Chinese restaurants, and sometimes, like underneath her nails.

The gums were receding, going nowhere fast.

Outside the dentist's the heat was a white glass sheet. Dusty cars blared their horns at traffic jams, fingers drummed roofs. She wanted to run crazy and smash the heat with her hands. She stumbled into a bleached-out park, fell on a bench and fell, instantly, apart. She saw her mother's dentures floating with a fat blue fly. She saw her father smile with his lips held taut, like his plate would spin out and into space. She saw old soft collapsed faces sitting out in deckchairs, their legs far apart. Her father yelled, 'say *Cheese*' and photographs reeled away from her: two and a half decades of smiles.

Twenty-five years old: down to bone.

No one would kiss her.

In the park, in the no-breeze, it hit her: no one would kiss her. No one would kiss her. She saw lovers in swim-suits. She saw kissers everywhere, kissing. She saw her face turned up and her lids going down like blinds. The air thickening. She felt emotions load in her chest and launched herself home.

No one would kiss her with false teeth.

Bare chests burned in her road. Diggers dug over yellow pipes and tubes, machines spun. A tiny red radio blared, not tuned in, a crackling disturbance in the air. She stamped up the pavement. She smelt toffee-apple tarmac and tea stewing in a little toothpaste-coloured hut. 'Cheer up my darling,' a big one said. She chose him. She walked up to him, so close his smile slipped. 'Come on then,' she said, 'Come on then. *Kiss.*'

His name was Phil. She could call him Philly. She could call him anything she liked, my doll. She took him from his little hut, down the road to her room. His mates screamed. His mates could not believe his luck.

She was twenty-five, only twenty-five.

She pulled the curtains shut and pulled in for the close-up: he had little black hairs in groups poking out of his nose and four pulled apart pores. His big rough hands were on her back, stirring it, feeling for a strap. She knew, seconds before his lips clamped hers, his tongue would be a slug and also have the texture of liver. Four out of five were like that: meat in their mouths.

But he was – gentle, his bottom lip soft and feeling like a bruise.

She lay in bed counting up all the men she'd kissed.

When it was dawn and grey stripes had come through the blinds and the house martins were at it and the car alarms were going off and Phil was still, heavily, asleep, she counted up all the boys, including kiss chase.

She saw two, then one . . . an identical twin called Antony. She'd identify him by the birthmark on his knee in the shape of England and his bright yellow cable-knit cardi. He was blond and brown and ran away from her. She had longer legs. She ran to get him ready or not. He was never

ever ready. He hid. He was a giant canary in a tree. She shook him down, pursued without mercy. 'KISS ME NOW!' she'd yell across the playground. She saw the sweet white spit on his lip, the tremble in it, the way his skin was polished. And he cried straight afterwards, fists balled in his eyes.

Jase. He beat up on anything small, insects, smaller boys. He had no mercy. He was thin and hard and fast like a greyhound (he probably died in a motorcycle crash, or a fire in a disco, something young). He smoked No. 6 in the palm of his hand, scrunched his face round it. He grabbed her on a school trip, in the Ghost Train. By mistake, he stuck the tip of his tongue up her nose. She had to guide it into her mouth with her finger. They both looked at each other. Eight eyes. A skeleton, luminous monsters, creaked out. Ancient mechanics cackled. Then, he took his tongue away. And never spoke to her or went near her again.

Phil rolled over with a snort, pinning her right leg down. His hand kneaded the spare on her thigh. His mouth was slack, open, wet. She leant up on one elbow for an in-depth look. Not fair, still had all his gums, not fair, big square, deeply-rooted teeth, four metal fillings.

She fell back on the pillows, floated off. Boys and men jogged past her eyes, mouths smudged like charcoal.

Duncan, French kissed like a lizard and McDermod who sucked on her neck till it hurt, who gave her a necklace of bites she wore under shiny polo neck jumpers. Her friends said, 'Been babysitting have we?' And Ian 'monster' Sky whose nice eyes and nice lips lay on a carpet of spots, but who wiggled when he walked, snake hips, who had 'pull'. They'd snog at the top of her road, she'd run home straight after, show him the soles of her shoes, and gargle and scrub her face with medicated soap as though the pustules had split and were taking over her face like something crazy from Space.

Spud. Serious and quiet, a medical student, he liked his white coat, wore it on dates, pretended he'd forgotten he was wearing it. His fountain pens pressed on her breasts. He treated her mouth like a cleaned-out wound, lips working out the neatest cross-stitch.

Bill. A wide mouth, teeth like a set from a dolphin. Smoked, his tongue like an emery board under water, the gaps in his teeth sedimented and sour, he could do it for hours. The stubble on his face made her chin red so her dad turned away from her and all her friends knew 'what you've been doing'.

Jimmy. No lips, the nipper, fastidious. He wouldn't put his tongue in her. She didn't want his tongue in her. He nipped and bit. He didn't like a mess, he didn't like anything wet. He did as much as he had to and no more.

Dick. Like his name. The grabber. He'd lunge for her neck, fistful of hair and tear her to him. Pulled her into his mouth, all of her, ankles and feet disappearing.

Harry. Urgent in the nose, he'd make snorting noises, he went straight down her throat, dirty and fast.

John. Spend hours on the approach, first one eye, then the other eye, then cross-eyed, the space he'd eat between their mouths, make it like a long neck-nuzzling horse.

And, alone at a party, seriously drunk, her hair and body damp with dancing, she wiggled around a strobe-lit room. Turning a corner someone with no name pulled her up against a wall, roughly and dryly moved all over her face. She felt a beard, wiry. It was all – rude. Left her without breath, spun on the wall.

It wasn't a long list really, mostly boys. No one would kiss her with false teeth, no one.

She stood in Philly's vest, it smelt of concrete dust, dried yellow-onion sweat, brushing at her teeth. Outside, she heard the diggers vibrating the road. Vibrations tingled under her toes. The mirror was old and tinted and flattered the mesh of her hair and her distant face. The toothpaste gave her a foaming smile. She looked rosy, young. She was too young . . . could not happen to her. Her eyes swam. She tasted blood down her throat. Phil pinched her, said, 'Well girly, got to hit the road,' grinned, his reflection big and brown and black, his body hair a scrawl of acrylic, his body stuffed too full with blood, like the colour stuffed in a horse. You wouldn't think he could kiss. You wouldn't think that at all.

She kissed him. She wouldn't let him go. She followed him down the hall. He said, 'Hey, let go . . . '

She was only twenty-five.

She hadn't kissed properly yet.

He said 'Oy, *get* . . . '

She followed him down the road to work.

POSTCARDS

And my mother does not sleep at all. And I do not
know where my dad is.

WE GET POSTCARDS but they are from different places
and, sometimes, different lands. It is all lands, there are no
people or farms or houses. It is scrubland and coloured
hills. There is a man somewhere, or a woman, and that is
a job, to paint light and cheer up the country. And some of
them are funny. There are blue trees and green skies and
some of the clouds have faces. So I think it is the boredom.
They must get carried away. And my mother has a boxload.
To her they are like love letters. I do not understand this.
There is no love there that I can see. I have three of my
own. They all say, 'Hope you're keeping well.' They arrive
on my birthday. Not a day early or a day late. On the right
day. I suppose that might be love but I think it is good
timing.

And I am the last one now. My sisters have gone and my
brother. They have gone Over There, across the water. My
mother says they could not wait to Get Out, to Get Away.
She says not to mind but I do. The house is very quiet. And
in the post come cheques and money orders. My mother

will not cash them. And she tears them up into very tiny pieces. She shakes when she does this and hides the pieces in a drawer. 'I would not give them the pleasure,' she says, 'I would not.' I would. I do not see where the pleasure lies but I cannot say that. I cannot say very much to her.

And they went away on boats and planes so I am the only one left now. And one day I will go, though my mother does not know this yet. There are things you must do first. You need money to leave and exams if you are to get on. That is what Mrs Kinny used to say, 'Exam grades are Passports,' she said, 'that or a rich daddy.' But I do not know where my dad is. Mrs Kinny said I have a good brain and I could go far. Mrs Kinny said I must study hard. She liked me a lot. She liked all the unpopular girls because we did not play a lot. And not with each other. I do not have much time to study now. My mother gives me work to do as I am the only one left. She could not do without me, she says, I am her Love and she kisses me and pulls me to her. But she will not let me read or get on. She does not like my head in a book. 'What, with all this work to do.' And there is a lot of work. There is no denying the work to do.

And so, I do not go to school. Sometimes the Inspector comes but nobody can approach us quietly, take us by surprise. The dog barks. It howls and throws back its head. He has a rusty van and the road is not smooth. There are ruts in it and soft mud. And we can hear it cough and sputter and outside the house is gravel. And my mother puts me in the cupboard and folds a coat over my head.

There is plenty of time. It is my dad's coat. It smells of my dad and I do not like that. And she pulls a table against the cupboard and sits there. And she is a good liar. She calls him Mister and first he will not sit down or drink her tea. But then he does. She pretends I am Over There with my sisters and my brother. And soon they are talking about the bad road and the storms and the people in the town. He says she must be awful lonely on her own but my mother does not fall for that. My mother does not fall for anything. And when the van is coughing up the road she moves the table back and opens the cupboard door. She slides the coat off my face. BOO she says. That is our joke. And we both laugh.

And my mother does not sleep at all. She does not like to be still. She says she does not know how to be. Every night my sheets are clean. Every day she scrubs them and they are on the line and freeze into walls. And she stands over me at night. I think it is to make sure I have not gone away. She likes to touch my face and put her fingers in my hair. She does this very gently, not to wake me. And it does not wake me now. And I sleep.

And this is what our house is like. It is stone and square and has deep windows. And there is a wooden barn leaning and falling on it. I do not like to go in there. It is my dad's place. It has his things and they are all metals. They are tools and engines and old inventions and they are everywhere in the straw. They are all rusty. It smells of rust and the straw is bad and wet and that smells too. Also, there are rats. When they die they leak a gas and so it smells of that too. I think you can die of that gas so I do not go in there. The light does not go in there either.

And so our house is very windy. This is because the land is flat for miles. And the wind is always wet. It is a soft wet though. You do not know you are wet until you touch your hair. And this is because the land is swamp and this means that my dad should not have built this house because nobody should build a house on a swamp.

And this is what our house sounds like. The wind flaps the sheets so there are sheet noises and a shutter bangs because we do not go into the barn to get the tools to mend it. And the dog barks and splashes in the puddles. And it is my mother who makes all the inside noise. I think this is why she does not stop because otherwise it is very quiet. And it becomes still. The sheets and the shutter and the dog are not noises to us because we do not make them. And we have only two rugs and the floors are cement. When you walk on the floors the dust rises and you cannot see your ankles for clouds. And the sound is hollow. This means that I can hear her feet and she can hear mine. And she is always asking me to get things and to Hurry. I do not see where the Hurry is but she does.

And the things I must bring quickly are old. This is what we do at night. And she calls them her Young Things. And I know them all by heart. There are dresses and she holds them up to the lamp and tiny moths fly out and so there are tiny holes. And I sew up all the holes. And there are photographs which are yellow and grey and curl up at the edges. Of my sisters and my brother. I look at their faces but I do not recognise them. They could not wait to Get Out to Get Away she says. And there is no picture of me and only one of my dad. And the one of my dad is after their wedding. There are other faces in the back but they are blurred. My mother and my dad are young and they are smiling. And my mother has white flowers in her hair and pinned on her blouse. They are so white they are like shining lights so that is what you notice first. And that is because they are painted. And my mother saves this picture up till last. And that is when she cries and goes through the box. To her they are like love letters but I do not see any love there. And so I go to bed. And soon the house grows quiet. And it becomes still.

HERE COMES JOHN

I REMEMBER MY FIRST ONE. Nineteen sixty-nine. He was called John. A fine body of a man with his Go on, punch me *right there*, the reddish ripple of muscle, that covering hair. It was all over his stomach and all over his back. It used to crawl over his collar and out of his cuffs. The man was a mat, but I suppose some women must like it. *I* must have liked it. Before my brain grew. And isn't it the way with them, the ones that slap at first, then punch, then give you a right good kicking (keep you straight), it's all mouth. Took him two seconds with drink in him, three without. If I timed it right I could set my tea down steaming and after, after I'd cleared up the mess a bit, it would be just right. Very nice with a fag. And of course he'd be exhausted, fairly whacked, bushed. And it would be, Can't you give me a moment love? (oh, I thought that was one) or Jeezus! You a nymphomaniac or what?

And if you don't learn nothing from that you don't learn nothing.

Cos nothing changes that much does it? The Seventies, the Eighties, the Nineties. It all boils down to tit men (look at the conkers on that) or cunt men, or leg men. They still like to divide you up. And it don't make no difference if it's squash now stead of rugger, Bacardi not lager, they've all got mental hair on their shoulders, red in the middle, wee white legs. They're still all John. Old John and New John. And even in the Nineties, where it's all talk dirty, they still can't manage it, beckoning you over in a pub with their pinkie and off you trot, ever hopeful, and it's, If I could make you come with my finger think what I could do with my *whole* body. Or they'd spend all evening, and a couple of quid, breathing in your ear even though your hearing's perfect cos they've read some comic says you can do this and it's like foreplay and we won't expect nothing much later. Which brings me nicely round to John.

John was a fine body of a man, all dressed up. My ear would be that wet sitting next to him I'd have to keep swapping places for fear I'd get water on the brain. Now you're probably thinking I'm talking about some motor mechanic or builder as they're usually the ones with the tartan middles and luminous legs, cept you'd be wrong. I'm talking about The Johns. The millions of them. They're all stockbrokers, they're all Tories, they're all married (you put a scratch on me I'll lay you out) they're all BORING and so you're probably thinking, so why do you bother and my answer to that is, well, why do you think? Listen. This is how I met John.

Nineteen ninety-three. I was sitting in Rumours under a palm tree nursing a gin and thinking I could jack it all in soon and feeling this cold sore bubbling up on my lower lip, sort of humming, 'Wish I was pretty, Wish I was rich,' when in walks this bloke. Oh-oh, I thought, Here comes John. Oh-oh, I thought, a bit later, fourth gin (no t), John reads the *Independent*. Cos it's not all what's a gorgeous bird/chick/bit/bint doing in an etcetera. It's all uni-this and multilateral-that and IMF and ERM and ECU so you've got to read up a bit for these yuppy Johns and you've got to know your way round shares and things cos they might be tit, cunt and leg men but now they want *brain*. And *brain*, girls, is what I've got. See this necklace? John got me that. These earrings? John got me that. These shares in British Telecom, British Gas, British Steel, British Airways, British fucking everything, you name it, they sell it, I've got it, cos I bloody well earn it.

So anyways, to cut the eye contact and the, If I could make you come with my etcetera, there's John, finally sitting next to me, soaking my lug hole, boring me to sweet Jesus, and I'm doing my Wiggle On The Seat bit (they like you to wiggle, it reminds them of studs and fillies) and to look at me you wouldn't think my brain had just atrophied cos I'm well into automatic and I look interesting. You've got to look interesting! It's all Nineties clean, it's Anneka Rice. So what you need girls is glasses to take off and on, a lot of hair half pinned up and something collarless and well cut and that's me down to a t – with a gin in it. And don't get drunk. Know your limit. He can get legless but you've got to hold your own cos You Need Your Wits About You.

Listen. Here we go.

This is what Johns do. They come straight out with it two seconds before last orders, giving it the old Nigel Havers eyebrow and it's, I feel this strong attraction to you . . . and I think you're an interesting woman but I . . . I better tell you I *am* married. Pause. And then its the old spaniel 'isn't life cruel' eye dodge and the quicky glance at you cos here's where everything hangs in the balance. This is *the* crucial moment, so watch out girls, watch me girls and *learn* – get it off by heart:

I flinch ever so slightly to show I've got scruples and morals and I'm not *that* kind of a girl cos you see they don't like *that* kind of a girl these yups, they don't really like any kind of a girl but they do like disguises. Everything nicely wrapped up. So here's where I go all foxy and silent and fight an inner battle that is highly visible (they're thick – you've got to ham it up) and, My Aunty's Knickers, this one turns out to be one of those Who-Hurt-You? merchants and I almost blow the whole job. Gin goes down one lung and out my nose (I'm getting careless, I've had three too many) but still I *am* an artist so I splutter just in time and turn it into a sort of highly-charged sob like he'd hit the nail right on the head. It works. Of course it works. Off he swaggers to the bar with his tight little arse grinning through his Chinos and I take a breather.

What's it all about? you wonder. That's what I wonder too sometimes, cos what's a brain like me doing with pricks like him? But then I look at my bank balance and think, come on girl, you're getting there.

What's it all about? you wonder. What d'you think? It's about sex, like it's always been, cept now it's better cos it's about Safe Sex. *I love Safe Sex.*

Now these Johns are so afraid of Aids they won't put it in you and God, what a blessing for the thinking girl. You don't have to take your clothes off. You don't even have to let him into the house (I want you so much John, we might get carried away). All you've got to do is put up with an earful of spit, a load of highly dodgy right-wing conversation and act like you're dying for it – and the last bit's how you get your pressies cos Johns feel guilty about denying it to you. Makes you laugh.

And this is an important bit: Johns *love* romance. They want you to romance them. They get off on all that dark corner bit and putting on a silly business voice when you ring them at home (ring them at home, they love it, ring them in the middle of the night, they thrive on guilt) and they can't get enough of slumming it off the stockbroker belt, Del-boys and cafés, holding hands under tables. And you don't even have to kiss them – tell them you've got mouth ulcers. And what keeps the whole ball rolling is they can't resist telling their mates: 'I'm having an *Affair*' – cos what's the use in being naughty if you've got no one to confess to? And John can pretend he does IT. John is not afraid of AIDS.

Which brings me, horribly, back to John.

Here comes John now, my last John, my grand finale and it's swaying, it thinks it's got it made, it's sort of brimming and relaxed and it doesn't spill a drop, and here comes John now, thank Christ it's my last one, and it's lowering down and watch this smile play on my lower lip, I've got it down to an art it's sort of trembly and yes, it says, I'm all heart, and here comes John now and it's totally pleased, it thinks it's totally safe and listen girls, I am going to take this John for *every* little thing it's got.

TIME IN LIEU

YOU'VE GONE AWAY for a week. Up north. You say you want to get your head together and you may give up smoking. And it is almost your birthday and anyway you don't need a reason. You talk to yourself all the time, without nicknames, very seriously. Fiona? Are you going to get up? Yes, in a moment. It is normal. It is what people who live on their own do. And it saves on telephone bills.

You haven't got many friends. This too is normal. All the friends you have got haven't got a lot of friends either. As you get older you have less friends because bad things start to happen to them, like cervical cancer, HIV, freak accidents with faulty hair-driers. Quite a few of your old lovers are now dead or damaged in some irreparable way. You made a list. There is only one left. The one that moved away. Friendships have strings attached to begin with and then they turn to chains. When bad things happen to your friends it is like it happens to you. There is no point in courting disaster, meeting anyone new. It is best to keep a firm grip on the few you have and keep it careful. So, you don't have lovers now or meaningful relationships with men. Sometimes you just grab sex, like you grab fast food, and hope it's safe. Anyway, you haven't got the time. You are always very busy.

You've gone away for a week. It is not an easy thing to do as you are not spontaneous because you work in the Voluntary Sector and there is therefore a lot of guilt and stress involved – which makes you think you are invaluable and the place will fall apart without you. As it is you always feel you are running just slightly ahead of yourself. You have argued with yourself for a long time about this. Look. You are just one person OK? It is totally egotistical to think The Centre will collapse without you. Look, it's only a sodding week and you've left a sodding contact address, OK?

Going away, if you have money, and a place to come back to and a few good people who care about you, is a great thing to do because of the trains. And because time takes a stretch. Train journeys are great inventions and should be much better thought of. This one proves to be more than great as it takes four hours and the man opposite you has fine bones, green eyes and is a poet as he has a file labelled MY POETRY on the table between you. And long fingers. He dreams out the window and so do you, feeling a delicious wheel turn in your tummy as the grey towns fall into green fields, into golden stubble, into crystallised reservoirs, into a sudden wrap-around of fog which proves more exciting and fear-filled than the tiny lust bubble you've just formed of *taking* the poet, making your move. And then it lifts like an eyelid and you have arrived up north.

Up north the land is rinsed in soft yellow, brown, slate greys. It is a lovely late afternoon: cold and outside the small station, wood-smoke smells. The bushes and trees are naked with dress-shaped leaves crumpling round their roots. You have not looked, not *really* looked at a natural thing for seems-like-years. Waiting for a taxi you are quite content to fill your eyes. This is what you've missed, this quiet, this great big sky. This soft assault on your senses. How you wish you were a poet and not an administrator. How you wish you could stop this moment and just live in it.

And then you are outside his yellow blistery front door and isn't it strange? You have not given him a thought and surely he is your object, your destination? But, the truth is a little tawdry. Anyway, he opens the door, rubs his rough cheek against yours and settles you by an open fire with a glass of brandy and, then, homemade soup (you remember he loves to cook, is fussy with it), and two bottles of red wine, and then, later, a lusty romp on the sofa and over the back of an armchair. A deep sleep without dreams. Both of you in a twist in the old saggy bed.

Waking up you have grown ever so fond of him. The back of his neck looks nice and there is the same curl lying against his ear you remember from years ago. His back is pale and freckled and there is a small pimple with an innocent white eye looking up at you. You squeeze it out for him, very gently. It is a small act of love. The first of the day and the days to come. You have done this for him before, in another bedroom, in another time. It has a history behind it. You sigh. What is this feeling Fiona? Ah, it is happiness. I think I recognise it. You start to stroke his arm and make nuzzling noises and – isn't it surprising what you forget? He hates doing it in the morning, first thing. He is the one who likes a toothpaste mouth and a litre of tea and scrambled eggs first. First things first Fiona. You light a cigarette. You taste back-blown ashes in your mouth.

The day floats by and then the next day. You have been for walks together. He has shown you bits of His North. His accent is much stronger than when you lived together but you can still hear London in it. It gives you a pang. Still, from the tops of hills he points with his profile and with one arm flung round your neck. There is the village, there is the town, there – battling against the wind – are the hippy girls (really, they are well past forty), with straggly grey hair, toggles on their skirts, multi-jumpered toddlers with home-cut hair. You laugh your head off at them. After all, some of them wear flares. They are archaic, totally out of step. He doesn't laugh. He says he thinks it's sad. 'All of it is sad,' he says, sweeping the landscape with his nose. You think he's going to cry. There is a tremble in his arm as he takes it from you. What have I missed, Fiona?

You are anxious to repair whatever damage is there, the little rift between you. Over cream tea in the village you tell him what your life is like in London, in The Smoke. It feels millions of miles away already. You draw pictures with your hands, you feel him begin to admire you, fancy you again, and your voice deepens in the way you know is attractive. You tell him London is mad, is full of mad people. You lick cream off your lips. You feel him watch your tongue do this. You describe the view from your bedroom window (you live opposite a mental hospital, everyone lives opposite a mental hospital). You make an enormous metaphor, exaggerating the all-day queue at the bus stop: patients in pyjamas, their sad escape bids, nowhere to run to, the bus never comes. At regular intervals a warden comes out and ushers them in. Nobody makes a run for it. You say they look like sheep. You leave a sensitive pause. You lower your lashes because they are long.

Yes. You have made a connection with him now. You feel he has recognised you at last. You are no longer 'the old girlfriend up for a visit'. You are Fiona. You bet he wishes he hadn't left, let you go. You can't remember why you let go now. Isn't it funny? Yes.

He is tender with your elbow as he guides you into the pub. He is full of little jokes and reminiscences. It is as if you have not slept with him for years and years. Up north the beer is cheap and pours like treacle. He goes to the bar. You *really* fancy him now. You get instantly pissed. He asks, with a jokey leer, what your sex life is like 'down there'. You say you are a serial monogamist – or would be but all the tasty blokes are gay. You keep it light. You say you remember having a snog at a party in 1989. The truth is a little tawdry. You don't tell him any of that. You tell him nobody has the time 'for that'. 'And you,' you say, 'what about you?'

Well, he really opens up. It takes the whole of the afternoon and half the night. You rock him in your arms, support

31

him home. You run him a bath in the old-fashioned tub on legs and get in with him in waxy candle light. He is full of tears. You haven't looked after anybody in ages. It feels quite nice. The story is sad and explains the pain in his profile, a number of far-away looks. Her name was Mana. She was a daughter of the hippy girls and he taught her English 'A' level. And of course she was near being a genius and would be after extra coaching at his house. Love, he said, arrived like a tornado and carried them both away but, there is a price to pay for such happiness and, unhappily, she paid it. You are moved. You would like to know the cause of death but he does not name it. In the steam you soap and kiss him till you prune. Bad things happen to your friends. It is on the increase. It is up north too.

The next morning you bring him breakfast in bed. But he is fast asleep even when you shake him. You guess he is a little embarrassed and leave the room gently. He needs time to recover from emotion. Yes, he was the one who needed that. You remember. You go into the garden in your nightie with your coffee and cigarette. You feel a little let down. The garden, though, is a lovely balance of wild and tended, nature and nurture. He created that. You feel a bubble of love well up. You imagine him in your mind's eye, bending in an open-necked trowelling outfit, inserting a plant. You see Mana leaning on the doorjamb her long hair shining, her skirts filled out with bulbs and Biros, she is constructing a poem about him, about the space they inhabit together. It is called Intimacy. It says, 'I've used him all up already. I've *had* him.' They both look at you and turn their lips up. From a distance. Are you jealous Fiona? Yes.

The big winter sun pulls you up. It is white, hard and cold. Your forehead is crinkled. Soon you are pacing the garden. You are not at rest at all. And that is not fair. You pull the heads off some weeds and then you get down on your knees and tear away at a whole section. You think about Jonah and Jason, your enemies at work, and all the work they're sodding not doing in your absence. You garrotte a worm accidentally on purpose with the tea-spoon. You remember how evenly you spread the butter on his toast this morning. How you even heated the knife. You thought he'd rescue you, didn't you Fiona? Yes. You thought it would be easy didn't you? You've forgotten all the business of lovers: the coming closer, the pulling apart? Yes Yes Yes. You make an impression on the garden. You turn nature into nurture and vice versa. Your nightie, your fingers, your feet, are coloured in dog-shit earth. You are really *in* this moment. You dig and tear and bend. Hours and hours go by. It is like that up north. Time goes by like in any other place.

It is your last evening. Upstairs your bag is packed, downstairs you are dressed in your best and have never looked so well. Your diamanté flash and burst with lights, your skin is aglow from the clean country air and the different type of water they have up there. Your dress is never-worn–before and holds you in. You have higher heels on that make you feel tilted, unusual. It is a funny combination. It is doing your head in. Outside, branches tap at the windows, it is wild. There is a storm brewing. It is moving at the doors and the window frames. You have dinner (what is the matter Fiona? I don't know, I feel . . . strange . . .). He says, all of a sudden, he cannot live without you. He grabs your hand and sweats on it. There are less and less people left in the world. You agree. You list the friends bad things have happened to. You both feel terribly scared. Up north the world rocks. You cling to each other. You agree to go south and pack your things and move up north. Yes, Oh Yes. You make tragic love. You scratch and claw at each other. You end in a knot on the floor.

He waves you off. He has a white balloon and a red balloon and you both laugh and wave at them hurtling off in the cold northern sky. You travel backwards through England, to the south. Already last night is receding. It feels less urgent, kind of mad. You arrive at King's Cross. You have a lot of work to do. Grant application forms, a programme of events to launch. Lines of people sweep you off. You will write him a postcard. Time is short. You have that breathless feeling. It will take hours to get back home across London.

I'M RUNNING LATE

IT STARTED OFF like a normal Saturday really.

I told my mum if John rang or Andy or Eddie or Gary I wasn't in. My mum said, 'You're old enough to do your own dirty work.' I said, 'Well, I won't answer it.' My dad joined in, yelling up the stairs, 'So how many boyfriends has Lady Muck got *now*?' I said, 'In my day . . . '

He said, 'In my day, we only had one . . . '

I said, all shocked, '*You* had a boyfriend dad?'

Mum came in with the extension lead while I was diffusing my hair. 'What a surprise Tina, it's for you.' I gave her my look. I said 'Ooh . . . you-wouldn't-let-it-lie', I snatched the phone. I said, 'If that's you John Buckley you can piss right off,' but it wasn't John it was Sandy. Sandy, my mate.

She was crying. I heard her go, 'Oh Tina,' then she got taken over by a sob and the phone crashed down. What a drama queen. When I'd done my make-up and got a decent side parting I rang her back. I said, 'Oh no, really . . . did ja? . . . no! . . . would you believe it . . . bloody right!' But I couldn't really listen as – with the curtains drawn and the lamp on the floor shining up into my mirror – my teeth looked really yellow. I went and drew back the curtains, switched off the light and what a relief, it was just a funny shadow. I picked up the phone again. Sandy was still bawling, '. . . it's not fair, I only did it once . . . and you know I can't stand needles . . . and oh God *hospitals* . . . ' I said, 'Eh?' I thought, oh-oh, silly cow's preggers. She was off again so I said, 'Look I'm running a bit late today Sandy but, Sandy, Sandy *listen* . . . ' and I arranged to meet her in the arcade for a coffee and a proper chat-ette, cheer her up.

I had to go there anyway to get some new leggings for tonight.

When my dad dropped me off on the highstreet I was a couple of minutes early so I popped into Next (it's really gone down), and, when I was sure no one I know would see me, I dived into What She Wants and bought the leggings and a top that looks like silk but ain't.

By the time I get to the arcade I'm running a bit late and I see Sandy through the crowd by the telephone hoods looking well pissed off so I look like I've got the hump too so she won't say nothing. She's wearing pink Catwoman sunglasses, and a stone-washed fashion mistake. Trainers. I note them but I don't say nothing. Me, I wear black.

Sandy wants to 'talk' first, more like 'sob', but I go, 'Later love,' and pat her hand. 'Let's liven this place up a bit, God it is boring. Look how bored people are. Bored. BORING.' Sandy goes, 'Let's shop,' getting into it, and I go, 'Yeah, till we drop.' We go into Our Price first to have a look at their new boy (ugly), then The Accessory Shop. Sandy buys a pink bum-bag and a matching baseball cap and I buy a really *special* Mexican necklace and a pair of really delicate silver filigree earrings. At the counter it's obvious, the difference between us.

When we come out though we have a right laugh. We see this – nerd we went to school with, Ronnie Boyle, dressed up as the Security Guard in a big brown uniform, looking well dodgy. When he sees us his lips go, 'Oh no,' and all the colour drains from his spots. It was really funny right. He sort of side-stepped into these potted trees. Sandy goes, 'Ooh, isn't that, er, *Ronnie Boyle*' and I go, 'Nah,' studying my nails, 'it's a big lump of dogshit.' We follow him up and we follow him down the arcade and Sandy's calling out, 'Pin-head boily, boily boily pus-head.' And I'm going, 'Cor, hasn't he grown a nice bum Sandy. It's got *really* tight.' We march behind him like Nazis, Sieg-heiling and talking in loud voices about all the shops we're going to rob and all these bored people are well happy now and Ronnie Boyle is dead miserable and Sandy's going, 'Tina. If you forgot that Semtex again . . . ' I almost wet my knickers. We let him off by the fountain going, 'See ya next week then, Ronnie.'

They're piping in some of Bananarama's Greatest and we sway to that for a while and dance about as we have our fags. Then Sandy thinks she sees Sister Emelda, a nun from our old school, dressed up in a leather coat and silver leggings with dyed black, nylony hair, just like the hair on my old My Little Pony. There is a *bit* of a resemblance. The hair goes into Boots and we follow her, ducking and diving behind the counters, to see if she's going to buy any 'sanitary protection gals'. That's Sandy's imitation. Sometimes Sandy's deadly boring but sometimes she's a right laugh.

We go into McDonald's. I get the coffee and some chips and Sandy takes off her sunglasses and her eyes are squinty and in slits. She goes, 'Oh Tina,' and her head is right down there on the table like it weighs a ton. I let her cry for a bit even though it's *deadly* embarrassing right and she's really showing me up. Every now and again I say, 'That's right, let it out love,' and pat her hand. I've smoked two more fags by the time she's decent. Down the next booth though, there's these three boys, leather jackets, and one of them thinks he's God's gift and starts imitating Sandy and the thing is, it's really funny, I mean he was a *really* good mimic, like Rory Bremner, but of course I can't laugh even though it's hurting my lips not to. While Sandy's recovering and putting on her make-up though I go right over and tell them to piss off out of it. The other two are nothing special but this Rory Bremner one, he's alright, so I look at him when I say it and the other two are going, 'Ooh-wa, ooh-wa,' really juvenile, and this Rory Bremner one looks me up and then looks me down and just says, really low, 'Open your coat,' and it was really embarrassing, I blushed.

When I got back to the table Sandy had her glasses back on and it's odd when people wear dark glasses indoors because it's like they're blind and deaf. She was OK but a bit gulpy and her nose was a bit disgusting. She said this really stupid thing though. She said, 'It's funny to think I won't be around,' and I thought that was really just typical drama queen talk because she'd only have to be in a clinic for an afternoon. To take her mind off it I told her some things about the girls at work and more about this one girl, Patsy, who's got really long hair and knows it so she's always lifting it up like it's deadly heavy and oh-so luxurious and I tell her what Patsy was wearing *all* last week and that makes Sandy laugh. Then I tell her how this same girl, Patsy, and this other girl she's always going on about, 'my model friend', 'my friend the model' Murial, a right dog, when I went out with them last night and Murial saw her boyfriend in Cheers with this other girl. It was bloody funny. When I finish Sandy laughs but then the laugh turns into crying again, as I've obviously hit a nerve. I said, lying, 'Oh, come on Sandy, it won't hurt,' and these boys and the Rory Bremner one comes up and it's really funny right because this Rory one starts pretending he's a doctor and tries to take Sandy's pulse and he puts on this Swedish accent and the other two boys are being like robot nurses and I must admit it did really crack me up, though I did tell them to piss right off. Sandy gets up and tries to run to the loo but one of the boys trips her up, a bit, for a joke, and she sort of falls flat on her face and when she gets up one of the lenses from her Catwoman sunglasses is missing and she doesn't seem to know it so she looks really funny. She runs to the loo and when she's gone this Rory boy suddenly goes into The Fonz and starts calling me Babe and orders his mates to wait for him outside so they go outside and they're acting like bodyguards with their arms folded high up on their chests and he puts his arm round me and goes all Italian calling me Bella bella and I go, all thick, 'No, it's Tina tina actually.' So Sandy comes back and I say, 'Excuse me kind sir,' but he won't let me out – for ages.

When I look up Sandy's just outside the door and these two boys are messing about a bit, pretending everything's in slow motion and pushing Sandy at each other and going, 'Whoops, whoop-sy,' and Sandy's ponytail is coming un-done, she looks a right mess and she's blubbering again. One of them gets her from behind and holds her and the other one starts tickling her round the waist, a little bit rough. Anyway, this Rory boy starts lighting up all my fags and pretending like he can give them up any-time-he-wants, and he's got them in his nose and in his ears and a couple of girls on the next table are going, 'Look at that wanker,' but they start laughing as well. Some boys don't need much encouragement. Soon, right, he's on top of the table pretending to be Elvis Presley and singing into a ketchup bottle and it's really good and me and these two other girls pretend to be backing singers going, 'oo oo oo oo,' and swimming backwards. It was such a laugh. I mean really. Then me and these two girls pretend to be crazy fans and rush at his legs going, 'ELVIS, YOU'RE ALIVE!' Well, I'm going, 'ELVIS, YOU'RE ALIVE,' these two other girls, they're going, 'ELVIS, YOU'RE A WANKER,' but he loves it anyway and soon he's being Tom Jones with a fist down his knickers and a hungry Bob Geldof but the best one was his Jason Donovan on drugs. When the manager comes out with his staff I leg it.

There's no sign, typical, of Sandy and I'm running a bit late. Then I see quite a big crowd over by the fountain, quite a commotion. I think I hear Sandy's voice going, 'Help me, help me,' but I can't be sure as it's a bit noisy. I go to the loo, do my lips and scrunch my hair. The side parting looks really good, even though I say so myself. Then I go to the jewellers to see if they've got this new watch strap in. They ain't. When I get out of there I'm lighting up when Ronnie Boyle lurches past, pulling his portable phone out like it's a gun. When he sees me he stops dead and this big smirk stretches all his spots. I sort of *know* then. It'll be Sandy. Sandy, showing me up. He goes, and he's well pleased, 'Tina, wanna see something lovely? Over 'ere, by the fountain?' I give him the finger, pushing in the crowd, but even so when I saw what I saw, my jaw dropped.

She's only drowning in the fountain. The two leather jackets are in the fountain up to their knees in splashy water, with Sandy, my mate. They're playing to the crowd, lowering her head in and out like it's a yo-yo. Her shirt was right up round her neck, so it was bloody lucky she was wearing a body. I roll my eyes; it could only happen to Sandy. This little kid next to me is going, 'Daddy I *can't see*!' so the kid gets lifted up and the kid's going, 'I can see now, dunker dunker,' and everybody goes, 'Dunk Her

Dunk Her,' and they're dunking Sandy in the water. She's soaking wet already. The funny thing is, Sandy isn't screaming or crying or struggling, nothing. When I can see her face it's just – blank. Ronnie Boyle is standing on the rim of the fountain laughing, swinging the phone and his cap's right at the back of his head. His other hand conducts the crowd. Anyway, the boys do this yo-yo routine for a few minutes and everybody is chanting and I'm going, 'Hey, leave her alone,' but I can't really get heard. Then the two girls from McDonald's are next to me and one of them goes, 'Isn't that your mate?' and I say, 'Yeah,' and it was nerves really, but I laughed. The next thing I know they're in the fountain as well and I thought they were going to do something really funny right because they both bow to the crowd but then – one of them kicks this boy in the face, whips round and knees the other boy in the balls. The other girl sort of flicks her fingers under this other boy's chin and he collapses in the water. It was amazing. And they didn't seem to mind getting wet either. These two boys crawl over the rim of the fountain on to the floor and start crawling towards the arcade doors. It was all over in a second and except for fountain noise and Bananarama piping out and this little kid still singing, 'Dunker dunker,' it was deadly quiet. They carried Sandy out and her head and arms were lolling backwards. This big space was cleared for her. I sort of couldn't breathe. This picture comes into my mind of Sandy in the school playing-fields imitating Sister Emelda and another of Sandy in the dinner hall starting off a food fight. Before I know what I'm doing I'm screaming, 'SANDY SANDY WAKE UP,' and one of the girls yells to Ronnie Boyle, 'Hey, fuckwit, that better be an ambulance you're calling.' I'm on my knees by this time and I'm rubbing Sandy's hand. One of these girls pushes me out of the way and starts giving Sandy the kiss of life. I start blubbering. Me! I see me and Sandy in Debenham's trying on the wigs and both of us wetting our knickers. Then this other girl whacks me across the face and tells me to shut the fuck up and I shudder to a halt. Then, Sandy opens her eyes and looks straight at me, sort of through me, like she don't know me, turns her head and vomits up all this green water and bits of chips. The ambulance man and a woman come and they put Sandy in a chair, strap her down and carry her off. Then the woman ambulance driver comes back with red blankets and wraps them around these two girls. She puts her arms round them. Everybody is looking at me like *I* done something. Somehow I get out into the highstreet. At the ambulance the driver says to me, 'Are you coming?' and – it was nerves really. I looked at my watch. 'Oh,' I said, 'I *can't*, I'm running a bit late.'

When I got home I fell on my bed and cried and cried. Then I looked in the mirror: oh no, *centre* parting.

AFTER A DANCE

ONCE HE KNEW SHE'D DO IT, he put his foot down and drove his father's car through narrow roads, fielded on each side. She saw the house by a long green sweep of the headlands.

He parked between a tractor and an ancient box-shaped car. As he turned the headlamps off she caught a gleam of chrome and of dark leather seats. Birds flapped from the windows of the car. Hens. Her mouth opened to cry – the whiskey she'd drunk fumed in her throat.

She would recall that night often.

The house was dark, it had long passed midnight, yet the boy made no effort to be quiet. It seemed to her he made a great deal of noise – banging the car door, jangling the coins in his pockets – as though to advertise their presence. He had told her, whispered in her ear, the house was his Uncle's but he had the run of it; he was the favourite Nephew. When the Uncle died the house would be his and the Uncle was very old now and frail. He walked across the yard and into a thicker fold of black; the tips of his boots scraped stone. She could just see the white in his shirt. All the old ones had been dying lately he said; sometimes it happened like that. He returned with a large ornate key which he held up in front of her face. She smelt soil, rust.

It occurred to her to be frightened of the boy and of the dark house and of the man inside. She would not know her way back to the holiday home, she had paid no attention at all to the route. She shivered, rubbing at her bare upper arms. When he took her hand she allowed herself to be led under the low hood of the porch but she did not return his pressure. The key rattled in the lock. Then, she felt him bend towards her. The dark concealed his expression but she smelt the drink-clouds on his breath and her heart beat altered, he was so still. It seemed he might . . . His arm was along her waist. He was humming. Mock solemnly, he kissed her hands. She was back in the centre of the yard. The boy hummed a tune the band had played in the dance hall and swung her round so the skirt of her dress lifted up above her knees and floated in their breeze. He breathed into her hair, clucking like a hen, his breath and hands very warm, till she laughed and became easy with him again.

The door opened into a kitchen lit by the faint red lamp of the Sacred Heart and the remains of a fire burning down into a grate. A dog stretched ragged, pink-tinged limbs for a moment but did not rise. She watched as the boy blessed himself rapidly at the font. Then, smiling, she blessed herself too. The water from the font dripped from her forehead on to her dress. The boy led her through the tall kitchen furniture, and, holding hands, they tiptoed up the stairs.

Halfway up the house, behind a thickly painted door, a

man snored loudly – climbing and descending scales. She heard the sound of a body turning over heavily on springs. And it did not seem to her to be the frail turn of an old man. The boy tugged on her hand. When she did not move he began to whisper in her ear. Then she felt his mouth on her, large and wet. She felt his stubble burn on her chin as he half lifted her up the next stair. They continued up through the house. She heard behind them, the Uncle's deep ascending snore.

The room had belonged to his Maiden Aunts.

He let her in first, pinching her as she passed.

She said she could smell old ladies: damp, lemon and mothball, a faint tang of disinfectant. She said, wasn't it terrible to end up all smelling the same? He patted the wall for the light switch. The light – a low, bare bulb – blinked twice, then, it seemed to her, swung into light. It lit the dead centre of the room. Thick yellow dust drew back across the floor. The room was barely furnished: two stripped, single beds, two tall glass book cabinets, a square iron chest. Two armchairs sat in shadows along the wall. She asked about the Maiden Aunts. He said they'd died the year before. She said, walking in, pointing out tracks on the lino, wasn't it terrible to be old and make the same journey every day? She said she wasn't looking forward to it. She asked – He said it was a long story. He would tell her more about them in the morning. They could do all the talking in the morning. She had to be quiet now as the Uncle would hear. He patted a bed and sat down to unlace his boots. The bed let out a tiny hiss of air. He allowed the boots to drop heavily on to the floor. There were no sheets or pillow cases, he said, they'd have to make do.

Slowly, she began to undo the buttons on her dress. The boy walked over to the iron chest and pulled back the lid. Her fingers trembled on the buttonholes. She watched as he lifted out a blanket. When he came towards her she said, very quickly, pointing out stains on the mattress, your Uncle's generous with his room. Do you take all the girls here? He threw her a side of blanket to tuck in but he did not smile. She pulled her dress up over her head. He was in the bed, watching her in her underwear. She tugged the ribbon out of her hair. Under the hard light she felt – exposed and would have turned it off but it seemed . . . after the way they'd been together in the car. A creak on the staircase decided it for her. She was in the bed with him. He was laughing at her: did she think it was his bad old Uncle . . . *listening*? Still smiling, he climbed on top of her. The bed creaked. It seemed to her it creaked out of time with their movements. It was not like the promise of it in the dance hall or in the car. In the car, it was warm from the heater and their quick breathing. The radio played green and yellow on their skin. He said –

She heard but she could not retain his words. He snapped something at her and then fell heavily on top of her, asleep. It was as though he'd struck her and then been struck unconscious himself. The whole of his weight pushed into her collar bone. One of his hands lay tangled in her hair.

She lay under him, stunned. What was it that he'd said? She
began to cry. She heaved him over and sat up and looked
at the four corners of the room, the four, blurring, yellow
mounds of dust, and back at the boy in the bed. Dust
tumbled across the floor. And she was on the other bed,
unable to suppress her noise and then unable to believe *she*
was the one making the noise. Perhaps she had drunk more
than she'd thought? When she raised her head, it was to the
sounds of his whistling snores. Her eyes ached. Her hands
and feet were frozen. Shivering, she went over to the chest.
The blanket she pulled out was damp and so heavy, as
though it could break her under its weight. She was
lowering the lid of the chest down when she caught a
flicker of green-white: a deep pile of linen sheets, pillow
cases with lace edgings; her fingers felt along raised, em-
broidered writing. So, she was not good enough for sheets.
She looked over at him, at the side of his long hair, the top
of his shoulder, the spread of him under the rough blanket,
and felt a spuming hatred. She slammed the lid of the chest
down, but he did not wake.

She would recall that night often. What was it that he'd
said? She did not sleep. She listened to the boy's snores and,
from the room below, the snores of the Uncle. She tried to
turn the light off but the connection with the switch had
snapped. All night the light burned. At one time she stood
up for a book from the glass cabinets but found them both
locked. The small glass panes were smudged with finger-
prints. At another time she stood at the window watching

the light change the colour of his father's car, the rusty scales of the tractor, the glittering chrome and brass and mirrors of the Uncle's car, the road and hills outside and beyond them a line of mountains coming out of the mist. At last she heard doors opening and closing, the rattle of a tin bucket. A close morning cough. She saw two black hens race across the yard, a shine holding on to their backs. Dressed, she lay on the bed with her hands folded neatly on her lap, waiting for him to wake.

They sat at the breakfast table. He played with the dog, making it beg for scraps while the Uncle served a fry-up from the stove – eggs, bacon, black pudding – shuffling from the table to the stove in carpet slippers. The sound of them all eating. The Uncle asked was she enjoying her holiday and she said that she was.

DON'T GIVE NOTHING

MY MAMMY USED TO TELL ME, 'You don't give nothing away girl, you don't give nothing,' and that was how I was brought up, dragged up some say, and that was when she'd caught me in the field lifting my skirt up high for Macka and Sam. They'd sort of teased me into it. I'd said No at first but that was before they gave me the cider. Said it came from apples and there ain't no stuff in apples. And it was that hot it made you woozy anyway, like you hear, drunk with the heat. And my head was spinning with all the teasing they were giving – Macka's *eyes* – and it seemed like something and nothing to do. But Mammy was on me in a pounce. My ear bled for days from the way she clipped me, practically tore my whole head off. Mammy was a small woman, she had birdy bones but she picked me up like I was the kitten, carried me back over the field, over the yard and flung me into the kitchen.

But that was all the fury in her, boiling up and up like milk does, over and cooling, one blow and then she'd talk me down, talk me down with story, make me see the way of it.

So my Mammy was always saying, once I'd hit the age, 'You don't give nothing away girl, you don't give nothing,' and I'd squat on the floor with the kitten and watch her (she'd weigh every word down with work) she'd bang out the dough and mix up some feed and while she'd be banging or mixing I knew she was thinking what story to tell me, what lesson I could learn from.

When the window was dark, when it was black she'd say, 'I remember this girl – Marsha, we were tight at school we were like two fingers, hardly no space between us at all. She had a head on her so light with fancies sometimes it would float right off.'

(My Mammy would look up at the ceiling like Marsha's head was near the light bulb.)

'And we'd be out walking on our Sundays linked up with our shoes so shiny and smart as paint and she'd be telling one thing, something ordinary like how the dog had stopped cringing and howling like something beat up, or how her Mammy's jam hadn't set over nothing when she couldn't seem to bear how ordinary it was and suddenly that dog had grown wings, first really little ones, like extra toes, and then one morning the kitchen had been full of a great flapping and there past Marsha's window was the dog shooting away on angel wings. And the jam! You wouldn't think anyone could make a story over running jam if you didn't know Marsha but that Marsha she had the jam up all night dancing and swinging to some orchestra music – you wouldn't think they'd be room in that kitchen what with the dog an all testing those wings.'

(My Mammy would laugh; she'd fold her floury hands over her front and rock with it.)

'That Marsha. You know she could make the wettest most miserable day *shine* what with all the things she saw happening in people's faces *and in their yards*. You know, she could turn the dirtiest yard, the ones with the old cars in you know odds and ends, into a party place. If you peered in the old Bentley wouldn't there be a swimming pool there just for us to dive in and some old shed with grey hay poking out they'd be a gorgeous man asleep but chewing a straw.'

(My Mammy would look at me.)

'She wasn't a beauty, Marsha, no, she couldn't keep her eyes still for one thing, they'd be travelling all over, like there wasn't enough seconds in the day to magic with, and she was big you see, like a farmer, beef hands and those kinds of feet that have no ankles, real heavy, like she'd had to be anchored down. But that didn't stop her head from just floating off.

'A blue moon would come and they'd be The Dance. You wouldn't believe the event it was or the travelling time to get there. A haycart or a donkey or your brother's bicycle, or you'd hitch a ride when the sun was hardly set down just to make sure because there was no missing it.'

(My Mammy would touch her old apron, hold it out like a dress, half twirl.)

'And for Marsha it was like going to heaven, like she was already there and some old dance hall with the kids running wild and the old men at the bar already half gone and us young ones dressed up best we could and stiff with the waiting, it was too big for her, it was food for months of imagining and you'd think she had some bird's eye view the way she could see every tiny thing, circle and centre that old dance floor with her great eyes.

'So we'd be lined up, you know, girls on the one side, boys on the other and it would take ages before we'd meet in the middle, all the side-stepping going on and dancing round what we called our handbags but were no more than patch-worked sacks or something grander we'd borrowed from an elder sister and were trebly conscious of as they'd be hell to pay. You know in those days finery took a lot of gathering though they'd be lots of us with a hem turned down three maybe four times and though we might look fit enough it was shaming. And Marsha on these occasions was a Queen no matter what was on her back, no matter how big those shoulders and those feet planted and sucking in all the air around her – she'd imagined herself a beauty so she just lit up. I close my eyes now and it's no memory what she wore but what she said she wore. This night she'd imagined herself a ball gown stuck out with petticoats and off her shoulders and showing tops of snowy breasts and a cleavage and not a freckle but sequins thousands of them and she'd said it out so real I could see it myself and was afraid to touch her sleeve just in case I crumple and mark up that silk.

'There were those you know who teased her, thought her touched and there were those who thought she lived above herself and anyone that high-flying must have their wings clipped, must be cut down, so somewhere in the evening they'd be a, 'Hey Princess, nice of you to drop in,' and 'Lady Marsha, that's a fine auld sack you're wearing,' and it would kind of daze her, make her blink and maybe she would look down and see the real thing she was and it would leave a dent or sometimes she'd be so light she'd thank them kindly and take it for an invitation to the dance.'

(My Mammy would look at me, my Mammy would look through me.)

'To see Marsha dance it was like, it was like someone stepping into music that was always there and big as she was she'd be on her toes and light as a note. People would clear a space for her, you know it was marvellous, like she was taken over like everything had slowed to watch, not just the people but the air felt higher and the light turned something watery, sheened.

'And this one evening, there was a gaggle of us girls sweated up from our dancing with our hair beginning to unravel and our noses and teeth shining and under our arms moist shadows and it was about the time the boys had stiffened up their spines and were bridging that great space and pulling us out to dance the slow ones.'

(My Mammy would look at me sharp, thinking of Macka.)

'And just like there was only one Marsha half in but mostly out of this world they'd be one boy who was mostly man and some part animal with all the speed of growing he'd done.'

(My Mammy's lips are tight and whitening.)

'And this one's name was Matthew Charles. Two names and no shortening, nothing familial, not even when he was babied and his mother ten times the size of him. Matthew Charles you'd hear, like he was an Island or a Corporation, like he didn't belong. And no good girl would go with him, no good would come of him. And there he was asking Marsha to dance.

'You know, there are silences so long there's no recovering from them. I think it was in him, something dark and gathering outwards, like some terrible flower with a swallowing mouth. There's no real explaining it. He was opening his arms out and smiling that relaxation men have, not like the boys with their croaking limbs and Adam's big enough to chew on, but like a daring man, a one-chance.

'They had the eyes of the hall on them. Though Marsha knew the tales of him he was like an arrival, like her prince and her in her ball gown billowing to take off. And we were fast friends you know. She'd flung me her last look and though the space between us was tight as fingers I felt that drag and gathering, saw the swallowing mouth.'

(My Mammy would look down, the swirls of her apron, the fade there.)

'Matthew Charles I'd hear, Matthew Charles, his names rolling in and on her tongue and back and forward the lanes we trod, in secret now with nothing the same and everything gone. My own Mammy wouldn't give her the time of day, the whisper behind her back something fierce. You know her back was broad but she could not bear it. She seemed to come swell and plod and her eyes had slowed and there was no magicing the rain away or the mud in the fields unless he was there, Matthew Charles with his two names and her none.'

(My Mammy would go over to the sink, turn the tap and wash her work away, the flour or the dirt floor, and scrub at her nails.)

'He made her heavy see, where she couldn't bear the weight and there was no transforming it, no crazing it away. It grew and grew larger than her life and one day, one day her head it just floated away.'

(My Mammy would look at me across the kitchen, at my fifteen-year-old legs, at the tan on my bare arms, at the middle of my folded body.)

'You don't give nothing away girl, not the name you're given and not the body I grew you, can you hear me speaking to you?'

My Mammy would shake out the sheets, smack at the wrinkles, get me to hold the edge and fold and I knew she was thinking what more story to tell me, what lesson I wouldn't learn from.

LOVE JOBS

HERE'S HIM, Steve, laughing, the afternoon after, tearing and screwing up wrapping paper, missing the bin by three yards of carpet. So far they've got: one fondue set, one glass fish, two toasters, five sets of towels, three double duvet covers, a crystallised punch bowl, four sets of darts, two sets of guitar strings, one plectrum – and not a lot else. Here's her, the bride, Gilly, diving at the papers, smoothing and folding them up – she's the kind that keeps. She's gone mad. They should have got a wedding list from a department store: they've got crap. She told him five, six, how many times? Her face is tight; her home-done high-lights fly around the room like sparks. Here's me, the Best Man, death warmed up. I've slept in my tux. She yanks the cushion out from under my neck. Here's him, 'Hey more like it, *nice*, from Eve.' *Eve*.

He's holding up silver, a photo frame, he holds it up in a sun beam, it cuts right inside my eyes. My shattered eyes. He drops it: 'Oh, whoops.' She goes for him. I go for a walk.

As I go down the hall I hear her go, 'What's *he* still here for?'

As I click the gate I hear a muted thump, a toaster. I hear her go, 'You ruddy . . . '

I'm halfway down the road when it's panting: it's Steve with his dog. He's in his vest, boxers and a grin. He's pinned Gilly's wedding veil on, it's floating out. I hear her squeal, 'Bring that back . . . or . . . ' Steve hands me Muttley like a bag. 'Take her walkies Joey, or she'll kill it.' And he's backing up the road. And he's in the house. I think – married: that's my one mate gone; that's the end of that.

Here's me down on the tow path, by the canal. It's not pretty. I'm standing on ginger leaves, flattened doggy-do. The sky is one low-down cloud of bilge smoke. The water is not water. It's black, still, Guinness, with oil on top of it, with dust on top of it, under it God knows, bicycle skeletons, skeletons. *Nothing* could live in that. If it wasn't so stinking I'd jump straight in. Here's me: hung over, hung right over. Somewhere, further down, a generator is pounding at my head. I've got to find a dead quiet place, do a think about her, Eve, my ex-wife. I hadn't thought about her in . . . five years. We all used to gig together – me, Steve, Eve: 'The Three Leaves'. I still can't believe . . . at the wedding, I still can't believe she just *walked past*. I've got to get home, get flat. I've got Muttley on the wander-lead. She's sniffing stuffed bin-liners, out on the slack. She crouches and strains and some dogs-do is so disgusting, it's hanging out like another tail, I can't look.

It's in the second I look away, out of nowhere, two blokes in black. I'm going to get mugged. I think, who cares? Then it's like I'm taking photos, rapid, action shots. There's a fat one and a thin one. The thin one, he's got

Muttley — click, and the fat one . . . he's got an iron bar — click, whacking it on his leg — click, charging up the tow path — click click click. Here's the fat one: 'Oy, Tuxedo. Give,' rubbing his forefinger and thumb. The thin one holds Muttley up above the black. The extra tail is still there. I go, 'Yeah, or what?' I really don't care. 'Or the bitch gets it.' Here's me, my best shrug, 'So, she ain't my dog.' And Muttley's in. She plops in like a rock and don't come up. Not a ripple . . . the fat one goes, 'Oh bloody hell Neville,' . . . not for years. The thin one goes, 'She wriggled I . . . ' And Muttley pops up, a flashy paddle to the other side. Halfway there she turns and doggy-grins. I doggy-grin back. Then her nails scratch bricks. She can't get out. The fat one goes, 'Look, she can't get out!' His voice squeaks up but I give a tug on the wander-lead and Muttley is back going yap yap. Here's me, I go, '*With* your permission gentlemen.' I haul her up. Snap. As I haul, this bone in her neck goes Snap, the littlest sound like snapping a twig, it don't seem enough, but Muttley is slack on the end of the line. Dead. Hanging there like a big furry fish. Dead. They look at me. It is quiet. Here's me, I can't believe this, I come — undone, I start to bawl like a girl. I see red. I see Eve's dress. The fat one coughs, but I just can't stop. He lights three fags all together, goes, 'Honest mate, I'm real, real sorry.' The thin one goes, 'Yeah me too, Gord, a man's best friend . . . If I could turn the clock back . . . '

The first drink is elixir. Like drinking gold. Here's us sitting on a pigeon-slashed bench smoking the fags. A dirty

swan is turning on the water, on rubbish. Muttley is
spreading out a puddle. I can't believe this. They are pat-
ting. I am gulping. My eyes are leaking. Every other minute
I get a hit on a flask. We've all punched hands. The fat one
is Charles. The thin one's his brother, Neville. Here's me
(repeating), 'Boys, this is embarrassing . . . ' Here's Charles
'Nough Joey. It was down to us Joey, down to us. We
feel right bastards 'lieve me.' A big shudder in my chest.
Here's Neville, 'Man's best friend a dog is. Never lets you
down, not never. Remember Redwing Charles? Bloody.
Bloody lovely dog. When he got run over our dad he
got upset, got a bit teary didn't he . . . ' 'Yeah,' Charles
goes, 'and you, you bawled your eyes out. And there was
that baby Jack Russell, and our Gary's Alsatian and that
boxer with the Boxer. He'd die for his dog, he said and his
dog would die for him . . . Plenty men go for dogs, our
dad, his dog, what and Elvis and Shep . . . ' Here's me, I
goes, 'I'm not . . . it's not about *a dog*. I told you, it wasn't
my dog.' I goes, 'I don't want to talk about it. You
wouldn't understand.' Here's us smoking on the bench.
Here's Neville twitching like a vein. 'It'll be about a lady,'
he goes, 'a love job!'

I don't need no persuading. I need more drink. They say
they'll treat me to this club their mum runs where they've
got an elasticated tab. I say yes. I need more drink. A motor
coughs at the end of the path. Here's us walking to it.
Neville drips Muttley over his arm. He's stroking her head,
shaking his. Here's Neville: 'When our dad brought Red-

wing home she was horrible, all mashed, lovely dog, lovely. When I think about her you know I go, I go all really funny, inside.' Then he goes, in a whisper, 'Joey, I ain't never told anyone this, but sometimes I go hard, you know, . . . *outside*.' Here's me, I go, 'Oh.'

The motor coughs in a throat of purple trees. Cardboard L-plates. The windows and windscreen are creamed with flies. On the back window someone has written OH KILL ME in grime. Here's me: *This*, I think, this is one A-class day. I have a piss on a tree. My piss is green and reeks of, what is it? – avocados we had yesterday . . . starters, some kind of dip. Charles stands next to me and has his. Here's him, in a whisper, over the streaming, he goes, 'I ain't never told anyone this Joey, but if it helps I've *been* there. My first and only love was Mara. She played the sax in my mum's club oh years . . . ' His voice goes faraway, 'Her lips. Her bottom lip was like arm muscle. What a kisser that woman, I still . . . ' Here's Neville, he goes, 'What? what?' We're zipping up. Charles goes, 'Oh shu' up Neville.'

We climb in. Charles drives, in fits. Inside we're smoking and sipping. My insides have melted, my headache is lifting. Outside, it's one long lemon-lit, blunted-building blur. Here's me, I'm wiping my nose on the sleeve of my tux. Then I'm holding my nose as Muttley is strapped up stiff, already reeking in the wonky heating; dead hot dog. What am I going to say to Steve? I can't tell Steve. Oh Christ, Steve loves that dog. What am I going . . . ? Here's Charles. He goes, 'We're not really robbers. You was just a one off, in the tux an all, it was all too much.' Here's me, I goes, through my nose, 'This is, boys, strictly one-off attire. Rat-arsed at a wedding last night, best mate's. Really I'm a . . . ' I stop. Then I look at their necks. Here's me, I was going to say, really I'm a musician, like I've gone for years – 'The Three Leaves' – me, Steve, Eve, then 'The Two Leaves' – me and Steve, now one – me. I goes, 'I'm a postman.' It comes out weak. I'm thinking about it for miles. Postman. Postman Pat. I think, that's what I am. It's not just me day job, it's me. I feel – whacked. Here's Charles, he goes, 'When I say we're not really robbers it's not really the honest God's . . . cos we are really robbers but we're not . . . ' Here's Neville, passing the flask. '. . . very good at it yet. It was my fault, I brung him down. We had a house an all, nice little bizz, nice little bizz, double glazing, complete window out-fitters, but I got a prob: dogs, debts . . . ' Here's Charles, turning round to make sure I know that is one under-statement. 'Under-state-ment . . . ' He goes, 'Dogs. He's dog mad.' He puts his thumb on the horn and underlines it, 'Dog dog *mad*.' Here's Neville, 'Look out!' We crash.

Write-off. The motor is totalled; the bonnet is halfway crumpled up a brick wall. What a miracle escape. It's sort of – stunning. Here's us sitting in there stunned. Here's us tumbling out. Here's them kicking the wheels. Here's me, grinning, feeling oh . . . Being nearly dead has pulled me right back up. Through the creamy glass Muttley's front paws are stuck straight up like she gives up. Here's me pointing in, going yap yap.

And I'm up all the way to the club.

'Our Club', their mum's place, lies below sea level, down stone stairs. Inside it's chrome, pink, gold, a round bar. Behind the bar a frosted hairstyle shakes cocktails up and down. Neville nods the word 'Mum' at me. I nod back; don't know why. There's so many women encrusted round the bar, on stools, all sorts, sipping. Shaking, sipping and kind of – sad. Here's me, perked. I suddenly feel well handsome. '*Hallo* girls . . . ' Here's Charles, Neville: '*Sssh!*' Neville stabs at a sign in pink ink: DRINKING ONLY. ABSOLUTELY NO CHAT FOR FIVE HUNDRED YARDS.

Here's us at a round wet table, drinking solidly, solemnly, at length. Lemon stuff, red stuff, green, purple stuff, sucking off the fruit. Here's me, I'm thinking loquacious. I'm thinking about the whole of my stinking life. I've never had a think like it.

Here's us, we're adrift, passing the five hundred yard mark, prising apart pistachio nuts, whispering over a huge, slushy cocktail, three straws. Their faces are pinky and sloppy with drink. We're just inches apart. Hundreds of miles away the bar is shimmering, glasses . . . women. I say, 'Eve walked right past me . . . didn't even recognise me . . . it was like a shock.' Here's Neville: 'The love job?' I nod. Then I can't stop nodding. Charles puckers up his lips and blows a red rubber kiss towards the bar. He's saying something but I can't hear. 'Here's me,' I goes, 'outside the church yesterday, being *the* Best Man, when this black Merc draws up and this glass-nylon leg gets out . . . ' Charles, he goes, 'Mara, her underwear . . . sweet, Jee . . . ' I goes, 'It was my ex-wife Eve. I hadn't thought about her in five years but I always thought she was always thinking about me.' Neville goes, 'Go on go on.' I goes, 'I just thought someone was watching for me and they weren't. I just thought I had someone but I got no one, nothing.' '*Us*,' Neville sobs, 'you got us Joey mate, 'now on. Drink.'

He puts a straw in my mouth. And, before I know it's happened, it's happened again. Here's me sipping here crying. Here's Charles: 'Ma Ma Ma Ma-ra,' his red rubber kiss pings across the bar. Here's Neville: 'Redwing . . . ' clicking his fingers low on the floor, 'Redwing, here . . . here girl.' Here's us, we're sipping here, crying.

URSULA'S ROOM

ALL THE WINDOWS in our street are moving.

'Ooh Jeezus,' my mum moans, fingers pressed to white on the glass, elbow finishing off the brown geranium, 'they've parked it in the drive.' 'And where else would they park it,' snaps my dad, 'on the moon?'

My dad has not been still for one second. Last night I heard him in Ursula's room, moving furniture, knocking knocking against my wall. I listened to him for a time and then I slept.

My mum is coughing, deep scratchy coughs. Also she is smoking, filling the ashtrays my dad empties. Our front room is full of dust and smoke, my mum crouched by the window in the purple dressing-gown, my dad flying about the room in his plastic Guinness apron pumping cushions, knocking over old cups of tea, the crusts of them shiny and green-furred lying perfectly round on our swirly carpet. My dad has not stopped swearing, bugger this and Christ that. Soon he will explode, the lines on his face rushed up, one vein ready to pop down his forehead. Sometimes you can see all the veins in his face. The blood is purple and green. 'Will you get dressed now woman,' he says in the voice that knows she won't, 'I'm going to open the door.'

'Clothes!' My mum reels round, the front of her dressing-gown smeary with food. 'Clothes.'

When my mum is angry her face takes on the look of a murderer, she spits out words and white flecks gather on her lips.

When my dad is angry his mouth doesn't move, the words squeeze through his teeth, his lips go tight and grey with the strain.

My mum and my dad look at each other. Sometimes when they're angry though, they both look alike. The doorbell rings and then it rings again. 'I'll go,' I say.

Through the bubble glass of our front door is a big pear shape. It doesn't move for a while but as I open the door a head jerks up and out of a policewoman's mouth comes a great blast of smoke. It breaks across my face. 'Whoopsy daisy, you've caught me,' she says, 'you haven't got time to kill yourself properly in my job.' Then she laughs at something through all this smoke that's still coming out of her nose and mouth. Her foot, I see, is grinding out the fag on our Welcome mat. 'Get her off the step,' my mum is hissing. There is a buzzing noise coming from the police-woman's shoulder. It is like a hiss as well. It is making the dust on her jacket jump. She is not very tidy. As well as dust there is ash on her front and her hair is falling out from under her hat. 'Well,' she says, putting her hands on her hips and throwing out her chest, 'and what colour are my eyes?' She shuts them tight and I say, 'Brown with blue flecks,' and then we both laugh.

When she's in our hall she takes off her hat and places it on my head. It covers the tops of my ears. Her hair is grey at the root and red at the end. There are hair-grips sticking up in it. 'And who would you be then?' she whispers, like everyone whispers in our hall. I point to the front room door. 'I'm the sister,' I whisper back. 'And they've been waiting for you for ages.'

Ursula's room smells different. It is pine freshener and shoe polish. There is also a paint smell. It used to be smoke and perfume and TCP. My dad has not been to work for three days. Now there is a white candlewick bedspread, a silk cushion and a teddy-bear propped on the pillows. A furry orange rug is on the floor with all Ursula's shoes lined up and shining. On the chest of drawers are ornaments from the back room: a shepherdess with a parasol, a dog carved in the shape of a vase. Ursula's Bryan Robson poster moved to cover the damp spot by the window. There is a lot of noise outside. The windows have been washed, but not very well. With Fairy Liquid I think. There are a lot of water streaks. We don't have net curtains. All the neighbours do but we don't.

It is nice outside. It is like summer and not like autumn. There is a very watery light but that might be the windows. Yesterday it was raining and the day before it rained so hard the air was full of leaves. Now the neighbours are standing on them and kicking them about with their feet. There are so many people on the pavement looking at our house. The two old ladies from next door are edging tartan shopping trolleys right into our drive, nosing. My mum would have a fit. All the women's mouths are going up and down. One of them in carpet slippers is pointing her finger at our front room. The man who's not her husband but lives there, a lodger she says, is shaking his head from side to side very slowly. Muslim children are running round and round the police car screaming and flapping their curtainy clothes. I rattle Ursula's window at them but they do not stop. Then I get one of Ursula's shoes and bang it on the glass. The other policeman doesn't look up either. He is leaning on the bonnet of the car speaking into a tranny. I cannot hear his voice but the tranny crackles and crackles and I can hear that. Ursula was always playing her tranny. It is one of the things she took with her.

I go into the hall and lean over the banisters. The front-room door opens. I hear my mum say, 'And how would I know.' She runs into the hall. I can see the top of her head and the back of the dressing-gown. I think she is crying. There is a wet sound. She is leaning her head on the wall. The bottom of the dressing-gown is shaking. Then I hear the policewoman's voice say, 'Now Mrs, now now,' and I see the policewoman's hand sliding my mum back into the room. I creep back into Ursula's room and sit on the bed. The bed is so soft I leave a big dent in it and my dad would not like that.

I know she has left something here for me. She did not leave a note or anything for my mum and dad but I know there is something for me. It will be under the floorboards.

My dad will not have looked there. I peel the carpet away from the wall by the bed. Under the floorboard is Ursula's five-year diary, pink plastic cover with a heart-shaped lock. I am just about to pick it up but there are earwigs on it. There are ten or more of them, arranged very carefully in a diamond shape. They are all dead. Some of them have leaked, there are smears of blood and yellow liquid on the cover. Ursula meant me to scream but I do not scream. I pull the carpet and the floorboard back quickly as I hear their footsteps climbing up on the stairs.

READER'S WIFE

THEY SAID it was a disguise, so I must have known he'd send it in – cept I never. They kept on at me to admit it, like I hadn't sworn on the bible. The wig? That bloody wig. It was yellow blonde, hat-shaped. I wore it when my hair was dirty. When Mum died I inherited it; that and the wall clock.

I never saw it you know, the photo. Rolf was at the end of the bed, we were pretty tanked up and I was undressing, giggling cos I couldn't get nothing undone and having to shush up just in case we wake the kids. And Rolf said, 'Smile,' whipping out his Polaroid, so I just struck this pose with my leg out and one arm dangling over the edge. The flash, it almost blinded me. It was Exhibit Three, 'the bedhead', in court, you know it was sometimes very funny.

Nobody would recognise me now. The stuff they give you here is shit, it blows you out, potatoes and porridgy things and all the custard you can keep down. It's something to do though so I eat it up, all of it. Five years ago had to hunt about the room to find me, skin and bone and nothing jiggling; smoked two packs a day and sort of picked at food, no appetite, what with the kids an' all. They grab things see, off your plate and that puts you off and there's always one or other dribbling somethin or spitting out his food – and then there was Rolf. Rolf used to joke, Mr Funny Man, cept I didn't think it funny – that I had two backs and that got me, that used to really get me. Nothing's fair. Now they say that's fashionable, clothes hang better, cept I never had nothing worth hanging up. In here, it doesn't matter what you wear, what you eat, it's like a relief.

You know, he was sort of pathetic, like one of the kids. I'd be going round the house with my vaccy, up and down all day, and I'd find piles of this mucky stuff, great big suntanned bums and a silly grinning face peeping up between. I always thought the girls looked embarrassed. At first, I'd flick through one when I was knackered. I'd have my feet up and a cig, but by the middle I'd feel sort of sick, like I was their mum or somethin. And then he'd come home – Rolf, and I'd get up and shout, 'What the hell are these?' and – you won't believe this – he'd *deny* it, shifting about on his feet. And once, he said the kids must've brought them in and I yelled, 'C'mon, Robbie's five and Jammy's six and a bit. Now is that likely, well is it?'

Men. Sometimes we laugh our heads off. We tell our stories see, these girls, some of them so young like they just got a Saturday job or somethin. I look after them, well some of them. Some of them are terrible, hard as glass, they'd stab you in the eye for a cig.

Rolf? He was, well, like a big dog. The hairiest man you ever saw. Not that you'd know that with his clothes on. He had this big, bald head the colour of a boil; you'd only know it by his hands, great hairy things and from the neck down like an animal. First see, I pretended I liked it – all that hair, but I've always had thin blood and in winter, you know, his body was so – like sleeping with central heating, with a very hot dog. His pet name? The Beasty. I don't know when I first started calling him that.

You know, I can't remember much of him. It's like a blank. I can't remember his eyes or mouth or anything about his features – just this incredible hair. Can't even remember what he was like when we were courting. He was just a man and he had a job and wore a tie to work and he asked me and I said yes and that was that. Kids come and I get wore out like every other woman I knew, like me mum and like me sister and like the woman next door. Cept I never took nothing, no tablets and no secret drinking, and definitely no going to the doctor. I was busy, I just got on with it.

They said in court, 'Diminished Responsibility', you know. This lady lawyer explained it, she kept hammering at me and what it meant really was, I'm a nutter and I'd get five years stead of life. Well, I got twenty. This lady, you know, she come to see me after and gave me twenty fags, 'One a year,' I said, and then she started bawling and I had to comfort her. Wrote me once or twice, and then she must've forgot.

Got that job see, in the baccy's, just a few hours a day while the kids were at school. Pin money, Rolf called it –

more like food money and leccy money and school dinner money. And it weren't enough, so I got one of those pool collector's jobs in the evenings, and that weren't enough, and I was ratty with the kids and had to keep dumping them with Myra next door. He kept me short. Had to search his pockets at night, trail of his clothes all over the house. Once, I found a tenner in his jacket lining. God, what a day that was – took the kids to the zoo and got a taxi home. Worth it to see those kids' faces cept they thought I'd take them every week so in the end it weren't worth it. They expect things kids, don't they – specially when they see their mates with new toys, new clothes, and I'd feel like screaming, Well, them kids ain't got Beasty for a dad, have they? Never did though.

This baccy's. Had fluorescent lighting, quite a big shop with mags all down one side. The light so bright it'd tear your eyes. And all these men'd come in and flick through the ones on the top rack, sometimes for thirty minutes. They'd sort of hover and get their courage up, and over to the counter and order fags and matches and a can of something and put this dirty mag down on top, like it was an after-thought. And I'd say, Three Pounds Please, and take the money and ring it up and they'd still be waiting there for a bag, with their eyes going all over, and I'd serve someone else and take my time, and sometimes they'd whisper, 'Bag please,' and I'd give 'em one of those little ones for sweets. Me and this girl Claire used to crack up after. The dirty –

And then I'd get home and clean up fore I'd collect the kids, and it began to seem like the house was covered in 'em, under the settee and under the cushions, two under Robbie's bed and, I dunno, I started to think, Robbie's watching me, he's ten now, and I stopped getting dressed in front of them and you know what, when I was bathing him, I'd look at his soapy little body and I'd catch myself searching for hair, like he was going to turn into Beasty or break out like a, a little werewolf.

I couldn't leave the kids no more with Myra cos of him, her husband. I didn't tell her nothing, couldn't. He started coming in the shop every other day, see, and he were one of the ones cept he were worse. Didn't know he was Myra's man, they were new neighbours and he's hardly home. Me and Claire used to do the paper bag routine cept it hit me, He enjoys it, and stand there staring me out. The mags he got, the filth, the worst, the kids and dog kind ordered direct from the manager, and he'd flick through them at the counter and count his change out real slow with his eyes on me, dirty dead eyes with no centres. And I couldn't sleep no more, cos I got to thinking, He's on the other side of that wall, and I couldn't stand Rolf near me, pawing at me. I thought, He's just like him, he's just the same as 'im. Maybe I should have gone to the doctor. I'd clean the house at night, tiptoeing about with rubber gloves on, standing over the flip-bin tearing them up one after the other, and every night the same, like he bought them wholesale, and I'd think, If he touched my kids, if he touched my kids.

That lady lawyer said I should have gone to the doctor, I'd have more of a case, and I were so sick I yelled at her, 'When did I have time, eh, when?'

Claire kept saying, 'You alright?' I was jumpy as a cat and he kept coming in. I'd hear the bell tingle and my face would go white, I could feel all the blood tightening in my skull – though I tried not to show it. He knew though. I'd drop his change, my fingers like ice, and I'd have to scurry on the floor with him watching, and Claire would push me out the way and say, 'Here you are – sir,' and give it him from the till.

It don't seem so long ago now.

Rolf was acting peculiar. All of a sudden he was saying, 'Give that job up,' and I'd catch him looking at me and his face were – frightened, and I'd yell, 'And what'd we eat then, eh? – dirty mags?'

And then, that day. That day, I come into the shop as usual. It was Claire's day off, so I was all on my own. You know, and all the regulars come in, one after the other, and there was no let-up, no coffee break and I had this head on me like it would split open. And then the van arrived with the mags and I had to hump ten parcels of them over to the counter and, like I said in court, you can't untie those knots with your fingers. So I cut the first lot open without looking at the covers and up the steps to the top rack and then down again and then up, and the bell kept tingling and I was muttering somethin like, 'alright alright, I'll be with you in a sec,' and I was cutting and stacking and cutting and stacking, and I heard this laugh and then another and, you know when you feel eyes on you. I looked up and down the line of them and he was there, and he was passing this mag to some bloke, and this bloke were looking at me and then at this mag, and I just knew what he'd done, what Rolf had done.

They said I'd meant to do it, but I never. It was like a dream. He came up to me very slowly with this thin stretched smile on his lips, holding the mag out. I'll never forget it, what he said. He said, 'Would you like a paper bag – Miss,' and some man laughed and my arm flew out into his chest. Inside, I was screaming, 'I'VE TOUCHED HIM I'VE TOUCHED HIM' – and that's all I regret, that and I don't see my kids.

GABRIEL ASCENDING

WHEN I USED TO DRINK I'd fall over like a baby. Lovely. Never feel a thing. This fellow – Dave? Mark? Den? – he'd get me here. I'd always wake up here.

This fellow at the AA. This fellow . . . He looked like a priest – wore an ankle-length black coat, face above it, clear blue skin, popped blue eyes, like he'd never had a drink in his life. Or been out in a bit of weather. This fellow who *was* the AA. Your original, radiant, Born Again. His real name? We called him Gabriel, Gabby, Gabs. For? Descending on drinkers and giving out gyp. Each meeting he'd drag along a new one and, while outside in the main hall the ping pong balls were pinging back and forth and these matrons were giving the floorboards a bit of 'ooh' and bounce, he'd be inside, whispering and urging, using their rhythm, trying to get the poor shaking fool to say it, what he or she is: a wretch. I've said it myself. He's how I came here myself.

His method? Simple. He'd spy you quietly sipping or in the act of falling over or catching a kip, sunbathing in the rain, in the park, and then, he would not let you go. You'd look up and there he is and you'd look up and there he is and the next thing you're here, propped up, bleating on this chair.

But not – It did not work on Gina. This woman he brought along, Gina. This woman, his live-in love. You could tell they were – And you could tell he'd been working on her and his angel act was just about doing her in. He dragged her here just once and she was just one *rude* . . . We all perked up. Leopard-skin coat, a sight of some kind of furry, black sheath underneath; tripping towards our little crew on these high red shoes. She wore her drink vapours like a heady perfume. No ruination evident. A dish and a bit. A *miserable* dish and a bit. While he was urging she was biting her bottom lip till I wanted to beg her don't you hurt it and she was scraping the paint off a nail and one hand was up her smoky locks and the other tugged an earring, and all the time he was right behind her squeezing his wings. But, he couldn't squeeze one bleat out of her. Lovely. Lovely to see. At the tea-urn, during the break, a couple of us were grinning and the atmosphere was all genial and light.

At the next two meetings though, he's not there. And at the next two meetings, he's not there and it's not the same without him. It's kind of *chatty*, but it's not the same. He was holier-than, but it kind of worked.

Just not on Gina. (I still dream about Gina.) I saw her one streaming black night, stumbling, screaming out of a pub, hands on hips, abuse-abuse, then clicking down the street in her high red shoes. And there was Gabriel descending, whispering and urging, being everywhere where she looked up. She looked up, 'Davey,' (or Mark, Den), 'ah, please, pa-*leeze* have a drink.' I thought: oh dear me no Gina, he'll get you. Oh yes he will.

Oh no he won't.

He fell. But, he did not fall like me.

My fall? Simple. I miss one meet then something happens and there I am one day with a glass and the next day, magic, it's a drink. Time goes fast – it's a wind machine tossing off a calendar. I don't give giving up, Gabriel, one more thought till I'm fairly rough, one of them shall-I-rain? monochrome days, and I'm in the park sipping, sunbathing, though it's cold and the sky's a rattling metal sheet and the willow trees have blown up skirts and the ducks are getting blasted about on the pond and the swans have got a centre parting up their white backsides. I'm thinking that that is a very funny sight indeed, I'm counting up my blessings (could have been born a duck), when who do I see? Gabs. My first thought? Oh Lord no. My second? He looks rough. Exclamation marks all over that thought: Gabriel *looks rough!!*

And the surge that went through me then was not Christian.

He was kipping on a bench, his fingers in a moist blue plait on that lengthy black lap. He'd been there a while – the way the tree debris had settled and the sparrow bopping on his boot. He looked – rough. I was thinking: now, with the addition of ivy he could be one of those green-tinged knocked-down blocks of statues in the cemetery, with a wing missing, half a face. My smile became a sigh. Why?

Because the mighty had fallen. Yes, I was feeling a little let down. A little bit sad.

So I let myself sadly and slowly down on the bench arm, got my bottle out and let the wine take different routes down my chin. And soon I was feeling, well, kind of companionable, all the cheery chats we could have now he couldn't flap his wings. I'd leave him a good purple inch. I'd give him a smoke. I'd be good to him and, important, *I would not gloat.* And just like that, as I glugged, I heard my own mother calling and a wee tale she used to tell above my cradle, head sideways on her hand: something about an angel and a mouse. Enough. Just enough for my two tears to let go as the bottle dribbled out. I like a cry. I was just revving up to me bawl when I heard a voice crack, 'Andy, stop that!' and I thought ah, ya bastard Gabs, a trap.

No, it wasn't.

The moment I turned my head I could see he had not fallen. He had not fallen down drunk. He was sick. Very. Sweating like he'd been squeezed. His pop eyes had sunk and they'd lost their bright blue blaze, and he'd lost so much weight he was almost one-dimensional. If he stood up he'd be a shadow. He stood up and was. It was like I was walking along talking to myself. What'd he done? She'd gone. 'Gina . . . tiger . . . no, don't go . . . ' He'd gone out hunting for her. He slumped along my arm. The one coherent thing he said was could I get him home. He waved a keyring at me – a purple and green globe. I thought, ah, yes, I remember the world.

Well, I got him home by bus. It was kind of a good idea at the time. I was *pissed*. There it was wide and red and friendly. He groaned as it jolted over the ruts and ditches in the road and hummed for twenty years in the traffic. And the branches scraping along the juddering sides seemed to scrape inside his soul. No joke. Oh he was groaning and making funny sounds and his neck muscles had turned to mush. I soon explained that. I got my hand inside his pocket (for the bus fares), and pulled out a triple pack of pills. A disease, in Latin, about sixteen names, swam at me, lay gasping on my tongue for a mo, then splashed, tail-end, away. Poor Gabby, oh my poor Gabs. I got my arm around him, gave him a manly squeeze. He groaned. Still, we might have been OK, we might have made it neat and nice, but in the next seat up an ancient fellow (there's always one fellow), puffed on a bugle-sized cigar – kind of defiant. I showed him the size of my fist, but he was one of those World War Oners long past terror. He puffed. The green smoke was a poison whorl. It whirled towards us. I felt Gabby's symptoms for him: the dry heave, the cold sweat, the top of the head wrung out, that runny feeling in the jowls. If you swallow it's – technicolor yawn. Projectiles . . . oh God, it was peas . . . How can a slice of shadow make such a mess?

The bus conductress thumped down through the steamy stench, unbelieving. Gasping, 'Bastards . . . my *bus!*'

I couldn't apologise enough. I couldn't. We were out.

The pavements were made of a bouncing material. It kept giving under my boots and Gabs was half-strung round my neck like a black overcoat on a suddenly hot day. He was babbling, then shouting. I lurched us from lamppost to lamppost. Fellow pedestrians passed on a firmer path (they must have had a map), swung their heads round on rubber necks and flung us looks registering through disgust. But, I couldn't register looks. I couldn't hold on to them.

When I used to drink I'd go with the bounce and a wave of euphoria would whoosh! and the pavement would rush up to greet me in a splendid red kiss. Lovely, like a baby. When you fall you don't . . . You don't feel a thing.

Every time we fell over, I never felt a thing. Gabby though, he felt everything.

His flat. Twenty – somehow, don't ask me – stony flights up. Not how I'd imagined it. Not exactly angelic. I'd thought it would be all bare inside, pin-lighted, aesthetic, black chrome. But no. It was like a junkshop with the lights out: musky chaos, shadows, a wall of lakes, hundreds of dark gold mirrors, some of them cracked. Old food stuck to one of them, a bit of plate. Plus women's clothes, sagging lines of laundry strung across the room. Was it possible – just the one line reflected? Probably. Soap powder, face powder, a mouse-coloured dust billowed over my boots. I stumbled over half-packed suitcases. Ghostly stocking legs kicked me in the face. Somewhere, fountains of books fell down. Gabriel was mumbling over my arm, 'Gina no no no . . . don't go.' I said, 'Shut up.'

Well, I was sick of him. I found the bedroom in a cave and flung him down on to a heap of bed and clothes. I was thinking, wiping off my sweat, now that is a job really well done. What do I deserve? Gabs was well OK: grunting in the gloom, making kind of pleasant noises, burrowing down deeper like a mole on its back till only the sole of one shoe showed and a socked foot with an immense yellow tower of toe.

I'd never been in such a sexy-messy place. I meant to take his change and leave but my reflections distracted me. Seeing what I looked like from behind, from side to side, distracted me. What would I look like without a beard? I was trying to remember if I had a chin. I went over to the stocking legs and made them kick me again in the face. Lovely. A shelf of pill bottles! I read his name, it was Dave or Mark or Len, one of them. Their primary colours and plastic gleam enticed and, looking for something to wash them down, I opened a cupboard: ten green bottles, almost-empties, sticky lipstick smears. Oh, the flat was a neat division: his crucial medicine; hers. And in my pocket I still had my what-if-it-rains goldy stash. Lovely. From the bedroom I heard Gabby babble on – the beautiful green fields, the gorgeous weather he was having and the marvellous view. Me too, I said and I floated up through the ceiling to heaven.

Oh, I don't know how long. But it was the best time I've had in my life. I came back. A bright spear detached itself from the curtains, hovered for a mo, then bored straight for my head. My hands (when I could look) vibrated at me, green. I was up again, on pulley strings, then down. The first thing I heard was my mother's voice: 'Mmn, cup of tea would be nice,' and instantly, in front of me, a cup of tea formed and sat steaming on it's halo. I've never wanted something so much in my life! (That is almost true.) So I watched it, wanting it, for who knows. Then, after the whirligigs, I felt all tingly, happy, off to the kitchen with something to make.

I was halfway to where a kitchen might be, when I remembered, slapped my face (*ouch!*): Gabriel. Gabby, Gabs. Oh no. And not a sound but, outside, a beep, a hoot; a far down traffic jam.

The air in his bedroom smelt brown, bad, tomb bad. In the gloom I saw his shoe, the long yellow toe, but I couldn't hear breathing. I thought, oh Lordy no. Then, his voice: the faintest rasp through the clothes: 'wonder parks . . . gardens, wonder. Wonder . . . ful flowers . . . ' I pulled off some of the clothes and found his face. It was phosphor-escent, slightly muzzy, as though he lay underwater, face-up in a pond. A dark growth, a kind of lichen, had sprung up all over his chin. At first I couldn't see how this was possible but he was even thinner than before. Bruises like bruises on old pear skin. I was thinking, now could it be three days? Could I have been . . . no. Was I up there for *four*? His eyes rolled back and stared up at the new light view. His lips were cracked, dry, but smiling. I heard him whisper, 'foun-tains . . . water . . . ' I heard him definitely croak 'drink'.

I was pouring whiskey down his throat when Gina burst in. She brought in white daylight, a square shaft of light that ran into the bedroom. She stumbled after it, crawling over the suitcases, calling, 'I'm leaving,' and, in a higher, mincey voice, *and yes I've been drinking.*' She was in that leopard-skin and on the backend of a bender, her black eyes smeared, an old argument boiled away on her mouth. In the white light her skin was lined writing paper, the cheapest. Ruination, alas, was evident. No, I don't think she ever saw me. I think she thought I was a side of furniture, a bit of laundry sagging off a line. She heard. She heard the bottle swill, her lines cleared, she laughed, 'Why, Dave,' (. . . etcetera), 'you're *drinking!*' and then, 'you're *back!*' over and over like he was the one who'd been away. They see-sawed: she hoisted herself up by his shoe; his sole sunk in the stuff of her belly. His sweaty head levered up, down, up. Oh, she was a purring leopard. 'You're *back!*' She sank. Delicious move; her big mouth sank around that yellow toe and – sucked. I thought it was just Gabriel, but it must have been me too: we went, 'Ah, aahhh!' She got to his face. When she got to his face her tongue shot out like a straw for the whiskey splash on his chin. I heard a rattle then, like rattling crockery. In that second he ascended, or the second before. I saw him get up and go up in a white, ankle-length dazzle of coat. And I felt? No, I never felt a thing. I never feel a thing. I was still busy thinking: mmn, where is it, where's it gone, where's that lovely cup of tea?

TAKING OFF

You SAY, sweeping, England will not let me paint (you like the sound of that), though your curriculum vitae is more than respectable and your shows pull applause from your friends. Everywhere pattern, you have to paint; why else live? Imagine, you say, if I lost these hands I'd paint with my feet or clench a stick in my teeth. Talent must out. But England won't let me eat.

Everywhere colour. Alizarin Crimson, Viridian Green, Cadmium . . . You say, listen to this one: Titanium White. The poetry of colour, a study in skin. Your themes are classic; flesh, your principal subjects naked; women, you store them in your head, stacked like dominoes. The world of light and colour is a woman washing, or a woman sitting and someone should plug you in. You grow, when you paint, the whole room glows when you paint, an incandescence.

Yet economies, always, depress (your jumper reeks of Vosene, the fridge illuminates a dish of phthalo green beans) . . . And though you say: me, I live only for the brush, you dream of being – reproduced and dragged, protesting, with held-up hands, to bat away the excess of applause, at posh openings as posh punters cry Speech!

Speech! You have *just* the coat to wear, bash the bottle on the boat, pull the velvet rope.

It is difficult to know how to live, when you're no longer young. Your bank manager though, is a (exasperated) friend and you clean, house calls, creaking up on a girl's pink Raleigh, for well-off women who enjoy paying a cleaning man and talk about you at parties – 'like living in a sitcom' – and turn doe-eyes on the grime rim in the bath and the watered-down Pimm's, the scabs of paint flaking on their parquet floors. And buy the odd picture and that is as much patronage as you get. Money, when it comes, runs with the dogs.

Salvation.

And not one second too late, and just as the creditors arraign themselves at your door, salvation! – an award of minimum status. Not much, but still it jets you off, allows you to clear your debts, to flick your fingers at your friends through the portholes as the Boeing 747 takes you away.

To America and success for a year at a tiny green-crystal University where students and faculty still wear jeans and jog between lectures, between white glass walls. And outside it's a panoramic technicolor in the smallest brush strokes.

Silence descends as you enter the stacked lecture hall. Your slides blaze up on the screen. The students and faculty are – rapt. Unnerved, your voice is a string unwinding in space. But, at the end, they stand – applaud. Applaud. And, *you like the sound of that.*

America.

America is wonderful and where it's at. You hear nothing, nothing but claps. Your postcards are packed. You list your (free) pots and pots of paint: Ultramarine, Purple Lake, hey fellas, a load of Monestial . . . Indanthrene Blue. You send jokey photos back of Me in baseball caps, Me in Bermudas, at steamy barbecues, in hot pursuit of someone called Suzi. And then, Suzis are in hot pursuit of you. You write italics: your letters detail ground floor plans; the campus spine, your apartment, the *heated* studio. Your space.

Your space has traffic. Students jog there to watch you paint. Life models *volunteer*. You never can get over that; clothes peel off on your floors. Now, you have a whole new series of women sitting, standing, kneeling, knitting. You are really somewhere.

They fly back with you to England and stack up in your room.

And, for a while, you think it will happen again. You will take off. Your friends applaud your new show. And time passes and you clean. And polishing black wood, sipping (borrowed) Pimm's you say, I have applied, but now England won't let me out. And that one American year burns bright Aureolin, Lemon Yellow. Ash White bright. Burns slowly, slowly, out.

HARP

I DIDN'T TAKE HIS REEBOKS, somebody else will get his Reeboks, it was the harp I was after, a *friggin* harp.

Let's say, it cost me something and it cost me nothing. It cost me me run round the Serpentine. I run round the Serpentine late afternoons, come rain, come shine. Got to get some cold air in, Underground out. You can die breathing this farty stink. I *know* people who've died breathing this. See those shapes in sleeping bags, in rags? They're not sleeping, no, they're dead. See, and it's my motto: you've got to keep fit if you live like shit.

I'm up to forty a day now, forty a friggin day.

How it was I was doing my system, finished up on the Northern line, and I was just about down, I was down. I was thinking maybe I'd worn it out, I had four pounds and fifty-five pence in brown. A year ago I averaged nine, ten a day. I had a system. You've got to have a system and then you got to work it. I worked the lines, one a day so Monday would be, say, the Circle, Tuesday Victoria, Wednesday Piccadilly . . . and then every two weeks I juggled them for luck. You've got to shake yourself down, keep moving. What I did then was I sung solo, two songs. One song to stop them, the second to gather them in. Up and down the line. Just had to open my mouth and the money poured in. Except you get stale.

So I was down, let's say it was a combination of factors, and I had this bruise coming up from this bloke, didn't see it coming. Caledonian Road he comes up and took my chin, thought, leave it out, and moves my face from side to side, thought maybe I could get his pocket. Thought seen that 'I Am An Artist' shit before. Gonna invite me to your studio are you? Gonna make me a star ya ya? Shit. Think I'm going to hang around in tan tights? Think I need a pimp to sing? Think I don't recognise one? But my timing was off and he cuffed me. Caught his rings on my ear. A while back and I'd have been quicker than his eye and off with his wallet and his watch like the wind. So I was holding my ear at King's Cross and I was thinking maybe I'd pick some scraps before my run and I was zipping down the escalator and I heard it and I thought, I've got concussion, that bastard's concussed me, but then I saw it and I said to myself, Hal-lo! it's an angel. It's an angel with my angle.

This fat boy was twanging a harp. He was pulling the strings out and just letting them go but even so it sounded fan-tastic and he'd got a hat with more takings in it than I'd had all day, a top hat, a *top hat*, and I started in with the elbows through the people and I saw stars and little birds twittering round my head and I thought *it* I am having. Having *it*.

He was dressed in gold, total. Gold jeans and a gold silk shirt, gold laces on his Reeboks. A gold watch he kept looking at. The stool he was sitting on, that was spray-painted tinsel gold. Beaming and glinting like a target.

'Hallo,' I said – I've got really good teeth, the front four are capped ultra white, cost this bloke a fortune long time ago, so let's say I don't smile for nothing – 'I'd give you something but I've got no change. I'd give you something as that's really made my day that has, that a harp is it, baby one is it?'

What fatboy did was stretch and yawn and look bored, probably had a million and one morons all day going, 'Harp is it? where d'you get it?' I've seen it. Probably thought slum it for the story, do it for a giggle. Seen those gimps in dinner jackets with their violins and their music stands, give me a break, and it was noisy as people were still throwing him change, and it wasn't even the friggin rush hour, *silver* change, and he pulled a couple of strings and let's say I was thinking, give the people a scale at least boy, and I matched them for notes. I just opened my throat, it's a gift I have, it's how I get by and I scat it. I decorated the harp with my notes. He said, listen to this, he said, 'Your voice been trained.' He was totally a-mazed. *Trained*. I said, '*Trained?* Friggin University of Life, mate.'

He was looking at me then, all Mr Marvel and I saw it. I saw my dinner on a plate. Let's say he thought I'm a story. A story for his mates. Spread it on girl, *spread* it on thick.

I sang. I sent out some bell notes and we did a little duet, a little bit of blue with a harp. Fan-tastic. People threw us notes. I just needed a little time for my plan. How to get the harp? Let's say, I surprised myself a bit as my heart was banging like I'd done a run and my left armpit was dripping. I was breathing like I'm breathing through a rag. I was just about to mug and go but then he upped up and he'd got a rucksack and everything, the stool, the coins, the harp, folded up into this little rucksack. He strapped it on his back – shit! Double buckled so let's say, he wasn't as thick as he looked. And then I looked at his eyes – bing-go! – and I kept up this humming so I'd got his ear cocked and then I knew he was high as I timed his sniffs, that neat little rich-boy nose was going to go. *Sniffed it*. Hallelujah. A shrimp brain.

Turned out he goes to music college. *Music college*. Turned out he was 'bunking off'. I thought, he isn't lining it, he's shooting his nose, he's probably thinking she'll have something. All low life has something. I'll have that baby harp boy. That baby harp will be mine. Told him my name was Bebe, know what I mean, tell them what they like. Turns out his name is Martin. *Martin*. Give me a break.

I said, 'Well Martin, that's a great name, make it up yourself?' Made him laugh, he'd laugh at shit. 'Well Martin, I'm not kidding when I say you've really made my day, you've *made* my day. What I'm going to do is, I am going to buy you a beefy burger. I am going to buy you a burger with chips. I am going to buy you a beefy burger with chips, with a cup of tea and with – the story of my life.'

Whipped him out of the station and over the road and sat him down in the Wimpy like it's my kind of town. I said, 'I want the works, the *works* for this man.' I said, 'No thanks Martin, I've got to watch my weight.' (No *way* I'm going to eat that moon cowshit, think I want a spongy brain, think *I* want a spongy brain?) I said, 'OK, for you, I'll have a cup of tea.' I dropped him some speed. My fingers were so fast. On form. Back on form and tabbed his chips. (I clocked the rucksack. He had it strung round his knee, twice.) I told him I love watching men eat. Martin loved that. Martin loved being called a man. Give me a . . .

And then he went all speedy. He looked at his watch like it was going to speak to him or decide to explode in his face. His hands drummed the table and slopped the tea and made the plastic ketchup bottles jump. He gabbled on with his mouth stuffed. I got my hand on his leg and rubbed. This is Martin's life story: Hendon. *Hendon* with his mum. And one helluva (Martin's words) one helluva coke problem, 'I just can't get enough of it,' (we laughed like hyenas). And guess, Martin plays in a band called Midas. 'That explains all the gold,' I said, slapping my forehead at cleverness. 'Right!' said Martin. (We laughed like hyenas.)

'Well Martin,' I said, 'your life story has sorely moved me. I will now buy you a dessert. I will buy you an ice cream dessert. I will buy you a banana split with synthetic cream and chocolate juice and you want it with nuts?'

I said, 'Well Martin, you want a coke?' (Oh, how we

laughed!) 'with a dollop of ice cream?' I had a hand on his knee and on the strap of the rucksack. I was fondling both. I said, 'Well Martin, we come from different planets. My life is on the mean and narrow tubes, picking and a scrapping a livin' an trying to keep clean. You like this Country 'n' Western style?' I said, 'Martin, this is my life story.' Then I gave him my full Bebe Come Home. Got him all *stirred*. I told him in my normal talking tone.

He'd got ice cream and burger all over his chin. Let's say, I sorely reduced him with mad food and drugs. Let's say it was a combination of factors. I said, 'Yo Martin, is that a Rolex?' and it's bing-go-city, sent him over the edge, *over the edge*. I said, 'Martin, I know we've only just met but sometimes a stranger . . . '

Turns out it belonged to Martin's dead dad, know what I mean? 'Martin,' I said, 'can I get you something? Chocolate fudge cake, maybe, a cappuccino? Milk is very good for you, it lines the stomach. A man like you needs a stomach-lining.'

Ever seen a face crumble? The nose was streaming, the eyes were streaming, the lips all helpless and the chin wiggled and wobbled, a volcano stirred full of snot, ready to explode under his face. I said, 'My Baby.' I rushed to him and put my hand on his hair and timed his convulsions. I kissed his forehead like a mummy. 'My Baby.' I said, 'Here let me get closer and get on your knee, here let me get that damn thing off you. Jeeze, it weighs a . . . ' And then I was sprinting to the friggin door with the friggin rucksack. I had the friggin harp, the friggin harp I have got. Zoom zoom zoomed across the lights. Down the Underground.

Forty a day I'm up to now. Forty a day.

BONES

THE HOSPITAL frightened them into it. They went the whole hog: relatives from America, an open car, church service with white dress, with white invitations, a singer (her sister). Simone arranged all of it, up on one elbow (a portophone, a sketch pad) during her convalescence. He didn't have to arrange any of it. He just had to be there. He really did think someone else would be there for him. Donna would stand up in the congregation and shout out for him. At the altar, he thought, like a kid, run, I can still run, his heart was sweating just holding her hand.

The consultant said, 'Both of you, calm down.'
Simone was lucky. They were lucky. Everyone told them they were lucky: there were complications but the growth was benign. The important thing was the growth was benign. Why? How did it get there, why? The consultant lit the X-ray screen. Nobody knows *why*; sometimes cells just find a place to grow. He tapped his pen at the cloud, clicked his tongue. It certainly was a beauty. He said, 'Both of you, calm down, let's get this into proportion.' He peeled a nail. 'Think of it like a giant moth husk.' Simone became hysterical. That was the second blow.

Euan looked at her and saw her crack. He didn't know it was over then but it was. Weight fell off her. First, her skin bagged, then it went all the way down to bone.

They did the operation.

They called it an 'investigation'. After the investigation, after they'd cut it all out, he rushed to the hospital. He pumped his horn in traffic jams, the front of his brain went. Hunched over the wheel, his lips began to chatter, soon get back to normal, soon get back. He looked in the mirror and saw his eyes were rapidly receding . . . dots. He screeched up the high street, the back of his brain screeched. He got to the hospital. Everywhere – red. His family, hers, had to force him to visit after that. But he visited in dreams. The same dream: a war in casualty, some kind of pile-up, rag dolls on stretchers, everywhere blood. He never could stand the sight, the tin-rusting smell, of blood. Through it, somehow, and in a lift, the further he went, the quieter and darker, his footsteps crashed, he held the bunch of flowers upside down, he tugged the petals off, he shredded the stalks. Her mum's shock looped on the intercom. '. . . had the stuffing knocked out of her, the stuffing . . . ' Following arrows, he found her, in a crowded ward. He couldn't believe it was someone he knew; she was wired up like an amplifier. Her eyes were clenched, her bottom lip was all tooth marks. He saw her empty; dead. He thought he should find a chair, hold her hand but he couldn't touch her. He dropped the flowers, ran to the corridor, one hand on the cold wall and threw his guts up.

He started to talk about it in the pub. 'It weighed four pounds that's two bags of sugar, that's this big.' He made a gesture like he was lying about a fish. 'Behind her ovaries, *behind her ovaries*. This scar, you'd think a fucking shark had got her.' He looked from his pint to his short, choosing. Hours. Then, into Frank's eyes. 'The stitches went septic. She had tubes stuck *in* her.' 'Gross me out,' Frank said, pretending to puke, 'gutted.'

She was so frightened her lips shook. She said, 'Look at this!' She should have warned him, she pulled the hospital rag up, 'Look what they've done to me Euan.' It was so disgusting he proposed. She clung to his hand, all knuckle, bone.

She said, 'Oh Euan, come closer.' He bent his ear to her mouth, the delicate hairs there iced, 'You do still fancy me Euan, you won't leave me Euan?' She cried like he'd seen nobody cry. To make her stop, to get out of there he said, 'Silly, we're getting married aren't we? Silly. I don't want anyone else Simone. I only want you.' But it was no longer true. He looked at her cadaverous face on the pumped-up pillows. He smelt her warmed insides coming through the scar.

He rang Donna from a pub.

Why her? He didn't know why. He hardly knew her. She fancied him though, obvious. He made rapid progress, got half a leg short of legless. She drove him home.

Why her? It was obvious. She arrived outside the pub within the hour, climbing out of her Mini in the noisy rain, the rain pelted her shell jacket and her too-tight jeans, her spiral perm, the smile she gave him full of dimples, pretty teeth. He told himself he just wanted to talk to a girl. He couldn't talk to his mates. You can't talk to mates. He just wanted to talk to her. He never told himself the truth. Sometimes they all – his mates, Simone's – went bowling together: Donna, Terry, Sandra, Dave, Tina, Frank, Simone. Donna was Simone's friend's friend. Funny, acting the goat, her plump rump, plump rump, the words were made for her, holding the bowl as if it would pull her down, her upside-down head between her legs. When she heard it was him on the line she giggled. She always giggled at all his jokes, made him feel good. She giggled when he wasn't joking. He made happy rapid progress. A fake tapas bar, fake Spanish waiters yelled at them. He drank straights. She would look after him, drive him home, drink up. She said, 'Oh you poor thing.' She was dead good. He felt how good she was. He said she must go to the doctor's. He made her promise. He told her pink blinking face about the growth behind Simone's ovaries. Simone's routine visit to the doctor, the internal (he looked at her to see how she took the word), *internal* examination. She took his hand. He felt tears. He let them go, felt himself come totally undone. In the Mini, on the way to the flat, he said, 'The weight fell off her.' On the way up the stairs he turned and hugged her head. He said, in her springy hair, 'You know it's funny I can't eat eggs.' The top of his head whirled round. He said, 'Am I boring you?' In the flat, he fell backwards on the bed, drifted. She drifted beside him. He heard her struggling out of her clothes. From far away he heard her say, 'Euan, don't let me sleep in my contact lenses.' He said, 'It weighed four pounds, can you believe . . . four fucking pounds. I don't know . . . don't know . . . did they weigh or . . . estimate?'

He started to drink. He'd drunk before but now he needed it. He showed his face at work in the mornings, at the furniture store, had a lot of mileage there, got through it, delegated responsibilities (made his assistants floor-walk, dust), then a bunk off to an old boy's pub he'd found where he knew no one, that was still good after the fifth pint, so extremely beautiful after the sixth: becalmed bar staff; a bit of still-life at the bar. A wave of fading pink lino. Days, weeks, months, and they still didn't greet him, not a nod. Brilliant. He seriously and slowly drank, fish-eyes steady, steady with his pint. Drinking there or lying in bed during her convalescence, hands holding his prick for comfort or, double betrayal, with Donna under his arm, he'd live their pretty, glittery life.

He'd see her striding across the Bolton Road. He'd watch her in her big girl's blouse, it's blue-white sucked in all the light. Her classy black bob, her bank skirt and bank briefcase, he'd squint from his shop doorway at the plastic name tag swinging on her breast: Simone. Wonderful, foreign-sounding name. Simone. He rolled it around in his mouth all day.

Simone and Euan, Euan and Simone: double income, no kids, two cars (a boy racer and something roofless), exercise bikes, matching mountain bikes, a Perpetual Year Planner over the fridge; trawl of magnetic arrows over the three years of their true love. He choked. Life was so good.

He'd see her . . . Her dark grey shadow parted cars. They met. She strode in looking for a bed base. He was bored, filling out an order, sucking on his shirt. He looked up and there she was. Simone.

She took him up, boxed him into shape, streamlined his blokiness, made him sharp and lean and neat. She talked – 'direction', 'getting on'; her Seven Year Plans. She made graphs of their future: felt-tip peaks; her thick white nails tapped in row upon row of green-lit accounts. This flat: the house after that. He was so bloody happy the store was a laugh. People liked being there. Coffee percolated all day, Danish pastries in the microwave, bit of piped-out muzak, not too much piped-out crap. It all went down brilliant with the bosses. They didn't know what it was but it worked. He laughed a rich, easy, happy-man's laugh. Their cheek-to-cheek beamed off his desk all day.

All smashed now like a plate, all bloody smug.

His colour changed. If Simone didn't see it, they did. His skin went from sun-lamp brown to beige to yellow to palest blue. Simone's mum came to stay in the flat, then his. He hunched over the TV set. His eyes slid away from theirs. All day they cooked and stocked the freezer up, ran up to the hospital with their small temptations wrapped like gifts in silver foil. They forced him into the car, made him stand over Simone, prompted him to chat. Christmas was coming. Christmas went. Simone stayed in hospital, one month, two. She had tinsel still hanging off her tubes. Her eyes were huge and black against the pillows. He heard Frank's voice laughing, chafing her along, '. . . like piss-holes in snow girl, eat that up, c'mon . . . ' He braced himself and strode in. He never mentioned the wedding, a date, he was trying to find a way to retract, keep it dateless, laugh the whole thing off. Simone looked up at him. She looked at him. When he left the ward he heard her cry all the way down in the lift.

Back from a wet lunch ratted. He was so easy-going the staff laughed. They knew it all anyway, Simone this, Simone that, every stitch. The first time it was funny. Funny Euan. He knocked over a shelf unit posing like a plant. His assistant's assistant, the lovely Jenny, very young, bossy, he liked that, he *really* liked that, rushed at him. 'Euan? Oh dear Euan, go home.' He sobbed, 'Do you know what they put in Weetabix fuck's sake, Riboflavin, Thia . . . Thiamin, fortified . . . ' He stumbled over a bedside lamp, pulled off the machine-lace cover simultaneously with his tie, and burrowed down the four-poster 'star attraction' bed. He belched distinct bubbles: whiskey, ginger, lager . . . gin. He heard someone, Gary, snigger. He'd get Gary. He'd bloody *sack* . . . The lovely Jenny tugged his shoulder. He peeled back a lid, her clean eyes, it was urgent he tell her, go to the Doctor. He said, 'Go . . . ' and passed out.

'Euan, come here.' Her mother sobbed. Her mother fell apart, took him by the shoulder, shook, 'You make her eat

Euan, make her.' Her whole family suspected him, he knew, of causing it, making *it* grow. He nodded. Now he suspected himself. His mum watched him. When she found the bottles under his bed she slapped him round the face. He let her beat and berate, throw names from his past . . . what he did to Sandy, Rose, Nicole, names he didn't know she knew. She didn't know Donna's. He wanted her to know Donna's. He was going to tell her so she could smash it up for him. 'I know you,' she hissed, 'you're just like your father, weak. You're going to stay with that girl, so help . . . '

What was left of him?

What was left of him crumpled under her will. The families ganged up, sat him down, extracted a guest list, a date in June. Then everyone went away. He lay on the couch. The ansaphone whirred with instructions, the dust fell heavily on the exercise bike, on the mountain bikes in the hall, on the empty breakfast bar.

Simone began to eat. The tubes were taken away, the drips. She was so happy about the wedding, she told everyone just how happy she was. She started to eat. He couldn't eat. He looked at his own gut, the water bag of it over his jeans. He heard it gurgling. The thought of defrosting something cooked, he couldn't . . . stuff rotted in the fridge, colours revolted him, putrid: red, yellow, greens. He went routinely, then not at all, to the supermarket. He read the lists of food additives, preservatives on packets, poisons. He wheeled his empty shopping cart down the wide aisles, the bright white lights pressed on the tender part of his crown. He wanted to get out of it, run. But he felt so weak.

Out of hospital for the New Year: wheeled out, Simone talking non-stop, waving her bone arms and bone legs. Now they both looked very sick; him back to gut, red-eyed, her so thin and yellow he could have lifted her and carried her for miles. If he could bear to touch her; which he could not. Simone did not seem to see him, how he looked, how he did not touch her. She could not see herself. She *liked* her new shape, he couldn't believe it, he could not. She stood up sideways from him, like a line. At the party, the Welcome Home Simone, she talked about the wedding. She went on and on: relatives from America, an open car, church service with white dress, engraved invitations . . . Her cake fork waved in the air. As the last relative left she was still talking; the bridesmaids' slippers, ballet shoes, what did he think? He got so pissed on sparkly he couldn't think; he passed out cold, in a curl, on the couch. In the morning she laughed at him, at his 'partying'; he could not move his neck. She was packing to go to Kent, remember? To convalesce? They couldn't sleep together anyway, her infected stitches, they wouldn't be able to lie down together, do it. She might as well get looked after. She laughed – get fed up. Her sister Annie's idea. He was so glad it wasn't his idea he couldn't look her in the face. He couldn't look her in the face. She went on. She packed clothes into a suitcase. She was bones. To get strong again. She would be fine for the wedding, they could save it all up (she squeezed him) for the wedding night. She would stay with Annie and Mike, plan a dream wedding, get a portophone, ring, write . . . send sketches of her wedding dress, the bridesmaids'. Time would pass. Get back to normal. Get back. At the train station she kissed him, licked inside his mouth. The back of his knees went. He saw her on to the train, watched its tail-end recede in a tight yellow space. A long sit down. Drink.

Then, Donna's pretty piglet face, blinking pink at him in a pub, then in her car, then in his flat. Feel her chatter break on his forehead. Her pink chewing-gum tongue peeped. Feel her complete body, stroke her plump boneless soft flower-scented skin, can't do anything else but hold on, stroke, hold on, too pissed anyway; but hold on, swiped by surprise every time, the deep soft deep falling down comfort of her cushion-covered skin.

Drum roll for him on the tables. Friday nights like old times, before Simone, with Frank and his mates. He'd get in their local gut first. They'd beat a drum roll for him on the table with their glasses. The count down. The wedding this, the wedding that. They'd yell, 'the yuppies come home!' Shiny rolled-up faces. They drank to 'the noose', the 'wedding ring' to 'boys on top'. They all laughed at that one, they all knew Simone was boss. But they wouldn't let him talk about it, the growth, bored with that joke. It was all like a joke. Keep your pecker up. Look at him letting himself go already, frog neck. Frank clucked his disappearing chin, said, 'You don't know how lucky you are Euan. The lovely Simone. You've got it made!' He felt his throat close. The words were there caught; 'I can't touch her, I can't stand . . . ' Drink drowned them.

He'd drink his gold pint down in one, seized by his, seized by his great swelling love for Simone. Simone! Outside the curry house his mates hugged him, hung on to him, slapped his back. Their sweat-wet running cheeks. Time to get home. He'd need to be home *now*. Outside, signal taxis in the middle of the road, swear ferociously as they sped past, empty himself out like a machine gun on somebody's garden, on their petrified rose trees, serve them right. Whee! Bang! His mood swung. He was so bloody happy. Sober himself up outside his door, giggling, fall straight for the couch. 'I'm too dra-unck to touch you, my lovely, my lovely . . . ' Simone wasn't even there. Ha ha, what a joke. A man comes home . . . He kept on forgetting, Kent, Annie's, dust. He swallowed the relief. Messages on the ansaphone. Donna's: 'How are you Huey? Call me.' He winced from it. Simone's. Her voice was strong and big, she sent kisses. She said, 'Love, only another week to go.' Kisses. She blew them down the line. He hugged his head with a pillow.

And dreamt he followed arrows. He was behind thick glass in an operating theatre, a sweating doctor, a sweating nurse. Donna sat in the congregation. Under the spinning disk of her hat she jumped up. He was making love with Simone. He was moving on her, inside her. He heard –

snapping, but he couldn't stop, losing his way. He started to bang on the glass. He screamed, back climbing the wall. Simone was standing before him. She opened her rib cage like a shirt and threw knife after knife . . .

By his stag night he was so oiled he could drink himself right through vertigo. Didn't see the growth then. A row of drinks in front of him, more lined up at the bar, his mates were spiking everything. Then, it was all he saw. The strippagram did her stuff – recited a ditty. His mates ringed them, yelling. She unhinged her bra, her breasts fell out. Under the club lights her skin had the glimmer of lard. He fixed his eye on her stomach, her plugged belly-button. He thought: in there, four pounds, that's my two hands put together.

Everything cracked, fell apart.

Train journeys on Sunday after Sunday at Annie and Mike's. On the last Sunday he told himself; get off the train . . . *get off the train*. He was pale blue and his hands shook from drink and not drinking that morning so his breath would be sweet. He was only fooling Simone. Annie saw, Mike saw, how far he had gone. The light knifed his sight, he wavered for a moment, punch drunk, then crunched up the gravel chips – a box of fancy cakes, sweets for the kids, so many presents. He walked in on them through smoke, dim shapes, a telly-lit room. Simone was saying, 'Ah Mike, stop, *it hurts*.' Mike was laughing, 'Well he can't – Richard Gere can't kiss.' They all laughed. They were all laughing. The kids grabbed the sweets. He touched Simone on the cheek, merged the touch with settling himself down on the gritty carpet for a day of it.

He watched Richard Gere kiss on the rewind.

Her breathing. Her hand on his head played with his curls, his whole skin crawled away from her touch, his whole skin crawled. He felt drops . . . one drop, two . . . run under his arms. In the blue telly gloom sweat stood out on his face like rain. And there she was. There – the image of her former great shape on the television screen: the swing of her big black hair, her glossy bank blouse. He saw cars swerve around her. In the stainless steel of their beams, he saw their life together in a shine behind her. Their life together a wide silver shine in front: all of it, gone.

'All turn round and greet Simone.' Cameras flashed. A white shadow, bone white, a drip of flowers, her big black hair swathed in lace. The organ squeaked. The priest meandered through the service. Then, it was done. They were out in the rushing light for photographs: air kisses for her, for him bitter-tasting powdered cheeks. He held pose after pose with her. Euan and Simone. Simone and Euan. Inside he was creased. He could not believe it, he still could not . . . Simone took his hand. He breathed quickly, quietly, but she heard. She put her lips on his ear. He could not move. He heard her smile, her whisper, 'Oh Euan love, soon.'

THEY DIDN'T WRITE each other letters, or phone much. If you're solid for life you don't have to do much. And they were blood brothers. They had thumb scars, white, raised, four-year-old little bleeders, screaming down the garden path. Their mums had gone, 'Oh Christ!' Thirty-five years ago. They didn't have to write or ring, but once a year they had a right weekend of it, down Rick's place, down the smoke. Len got on the train, swung past Rugby and Nuneaton with his Tennent's Extra and his instant mates in the mini-bottle beverage bar. In his flat, Rick straightened his cushion and his tie, all ready, set.

All the years before they drowned The Big Weekend in a sea of beer and wine, and beached, fish-eyed on the Monday, Rick teaching a riotous assembly God knows what, Len touting his cassette round the Go Away Clubs. They always had a great time. Gra-*ate!* Even though they could hardly remember it.

Thirty-nine. Nearly forty year old.

Friday night, they kept it local. And did their double act 'eh upping' and 'thou lassing', and shot games of pool in the pub. And woke up with the living room thick with sock. 'Don't you *ever* wash . . . ' Rick said, holding his nose, flapping. 'Don't start,' Len yelled, a wrinkled mole in the couch, 'starting.'

They looked at each other drop-jawed. They'd never got off on the wrong note before.

Six forty-five a.m. Saturday morning. Dehydrated. Might as well stay up, get an early start. Outside, dirty sparrows peeped on the glass. Outside, solid silver banks of cloud scrolled past. Outside a mad man screamed KILL ME KILL KILL KILL . . . Inside, Len said, 'How you can fuking live here, fuk.' Rick said, 'Jobs.' Then he said, 'I meant nothing . . . ' He said, 'Lenny? Fuk sake's . . . ' He put Elvis on, toast on, the kettle on and soon (after a smoke), the humpy bump was smoothed. Soon, they were well ripped, hee-heeing side by side, being little with the bleedy knife. 'Oh, Mammy,' they said together, 'we're blee-dy!' They said together, 'Oh Chroist!'

In the hall, biting gum, they squared up at the mirror. And froze over gap-toothed combs. The mirror squared back. Both had long lost their looks. Both were losing their hair. Both had pink skin-skids on top. The skids had got loads wider since last year's. Both thought, Gord, he looks rough. 'Why-we're-looking-gra-ate!' Len lied, like a (third-division) football manager. They paused. The pause went, they raised thumbs, hee-heed, and went out.

It was lovely and sunny outside, bright blue and breezy. Bright blue blasts of air. They raced down the high street like centre forwards, did headers into shops, tapped nifty finger work on their cash point cards: four saved-for hundred pounds for one major big bang bash. 'Show this country boy a good time,' Len yelled. He threw himself on the windows of cake shops like Spiderman and puffed out clouds. In there were, ah, jail bait. In there were hard-faced girls one-gloved like gynos. In there were girls who still blew up their bubble-gum. In there . . . 'Nay lad,' said Rick, he dragged Len's collar, 'Nay. Away. Let's not peak too soon.'

They raced to the bus stop. The bus stop swayed away in The Waste. Here, it was sad, bad, mad. Here, the stalls were chocker with dead men's cordless dressing-gowns. Miscellaneous bankrupt stock walled the street. Knackered black girls and knackered white girls clip-clopped home from clubs. Len sucked the smoke out of a fag in one drag, his eyes glittered like maniacs'. 'Fuking cor,' he said, 'fuking cor-ish.' 'Do you think this is me?' Rick said, holding up a shirt, swirly, not his normal brown. 'No,' said Len. 'Oh,' said Rick. 'Ooh,' said Len, 'Ooh ooh I feel like, I feel . . . ' He was straining like a baby shits. Rick knew that look. 'Oh Christ,' he said to Christ, 'not –' But it was far too late. 'SINGING,' sang Len. With a flash he had a finger in his ear and was warbling, with confidence, through 'Candle in the Wind'. Two of Rick's pupils sniggered past. A crowd coagulated: a yellow-eyed frothy-mouthed hound and a bag lady with black teeth. Rick thought, oh dear, what shall I do? He gummed support, hummed, and tried to vault a passing astral plane. The bag lady unravelled rags to her own larly-la rave-on, while a nasty thought raved in Rick's ear, and pulled him right back down: Len really thinks he'll get discovered, it's dead embarrassing. A drink-blurred memory stirred: Mind, it was right embarrassing last year when . . . '*Don't* take that off, Lady, fuk's sake,' Len yelled and he grabbed Rick's head and banged a tunnel with it through the crowd.

At 10 a.m. they were losing at the dogs. As the hare slid round, Rick said, 'Lenny, the yelling's new. What's with the yelling? *Eh, Lenny . . .*?' At 11 a.m., three hundred quid short, they double-decked it to town and did the galleries. At 11.30 a.m. they shared a loaded pipe in Green Park and a six-pack of really strong lager each. At 11.45 a.m. Rick said, 'Lenny, do you ever feel . . . ' He went on at length . . . 'cut out, bored, do you ever feel that this is *all* there is?' He was looking up through the rusting lace of a tree. Disabled pigeons dangled long white strings of shit. The sky had gone blueless. 'Nay lad,' said Len. He cracked a can, 'London's done yer, there's loads. There's er, songs, doggies, footy, curry yeah and – birds.'

High noon: they were rowing on the Serpentine. The water was a thick grey carpet with ruffled-up underlay. 'I don't know,' said Rick, gasping, 'me spark's gone. Sometimes I feel just like a song . . . No, I mean . . . ' But, too late, Len was cued on. Soon, splashes. Soon ten old, hardy, sparsely-covered heads bobbed alongside the boat. Ten heads hummed on Len's voice. Swans and geese rose up in protest. Rick winced the boat round. Twice he begged, 'Please Lenny oh please stop . . . ' but, Lenny cracked on:

Paul Simon. And Garfunkel, Barry Manilow, Elton John.
He started in on Sinatra, stood up to wheel about with the
mike. He rocked the boat. He rocked it again. Slimy water
sloshed in. Then tipped Rick and Len in. Right in. Everything went frozen and thick and quiet and deep and a
death-like grey.

At – whatever time it was, they'd lost track, they sat in
shock, in the dank boat house, peeled and steaming over a
tiny candle flame. Their damp green blubber loomed up at
each other . . . a distant memory: Trafalgar Square, fountain, same thing, tipped in, soaked, last year. Rick said, 'I
remember why you . . . you . . . fuk fuk fuk . . . ' He remembered more from years before. He wanted to say a
whole lot more. His jaw cha-cha-cha-chattered but, nothing else came out. 'Drink' Len managed, his lips belched
up . . . three, tiny black-gold fish.

Blinkless, they sat, crammed in a Soho pub, in matching
electric blue shell suits (bought, from the bold-faced boat-
man, for the fat, wet, almost-end of their cash). Their bits
of hair scribbled on their scalps, their toes squelched in
nylon socks, in green plastic flip-flops. Whiskeys and gin-
gers funnelled through their chests. 'My life,' Rick said,
'well, *our* lives actually, flashed in front of me like – *that*,'
he snapped his shrivelled pads, 'and it weren't nothing
much . . . then all I saw were wiggly old legs.' He went on,
'We're nearly forty year old . . . ' 'Burger,' Len said, 'get
me . . . suet pudding, curry. Chips. Fat yellow . . . '

They tumbled out under a low old-bruise-coloured

sky: ravenous, wrecked, they tumbled over stubble grass. Sinking, they ate in shadows, in Soho Square. The smell of hot vinegar soon drew crowds. Bony girls circled them, begging. People who fell over a lot held out scabby hands. 'This is fuking horrible,' Len said, hugging his chips, 'don't remember this from last year.' 'Me neither and I live here but hey, maybe *we died*,' Rick said, he looked dead cheered up, 'maybe we're in Limboland, maybe . . . ' 'Maybe you got a crack on the fuking head,' Len yelled, '*de*-pressing git.'

And soon it was black. Winter black and neon and car lamps and shop fronts cubed the streets: pink, yellow, blue, pink and yellow, black. Leather leaves and shiny rags from porn mags stuck on their shell suit legs. They rustled down a sex street in the aftermath of a row – their first since last year's big bang bash or was it . . . the big bang bash before that? Lightening grievances flashed. Loaded four eyes aimed, triggered, backfired. Both thought: this is well not fun, exactly like last year . . . or, well, was it the year before that? Rick looked at his flapping flip-flopped feet. Len couldn't help it, he just looked. His neck was a pivot turning his head into bed shows. From doorways leopard-skinned girls crooked their figures and their smiles. Len drooled, made like – Rick pulled on his collar. 'We don't want to peak too . . . ' 'I do,' snapped Len. 'Fuk off.' And he raced down to play down-down with the leopards.

'And um, don't come back,' Rick said, all alone on the yellow, grey, blackening street.

Hours of packed sleaze-horror slewed by.

Rick dropped his jaw as instant mates beat him up. In an alley, Rick was held, sweating, screaming, upside down, the electric blue arms of his shell suit were ripped off, his soft parts squeezed, change gushed like a simultaneous win on two fruit machines from his deeply-pocketed legs. (But, no flies on him, none: a damp tenner lay curled like an embryo, inside a sock.) Released, Rick waited, bleeding at bus stops, but no buses would stop. Coagulating, he limped along bus routes, his old, homey, thumb scar bleat bleat bleating distress.

By – and it was only 7.30 p.m. Knackered. And, it was Ca-hrist, fuking Saturday night! Rick was turning the handle to his flat. His hands and his bones were so heavy. His body ached. Tears shone on his face like two twists of cellophane. Ah, the couch to stay on, age on, collapse. He went for it but the hallway caught him short; assailed his nose with Radox and old, warm, over-painted radiators, a familiar Bisto curl of sock. 'Len?' Len came out of the bathroom, his face cut up and bloodied up, 'Snap,' he said. They both said, flat, 'We're bleedy, oh Chroist.' After a wobble, Len said, 'Er, what d'ya think my son . . . we get a curry . . . we stay in? Er, early night? Vid . . . ?

'Er, Rick?'

'Nay,' said Rick, 'Nay. *Away.*' They rushed out.

CERTAIN

SHE HAD NO PROBLEM attracting them and so was never surprised by attentions. She worked in a bank, at the enquiries desk, her bovine calm and thick, black, silver-threaded plait drew them to her. Her eyes had heavy lids. Her slow hands lay blood heavy, bloodily nailed, on each account.

She accepted all, reasonable, invitations in a spirit of hope.

But, nothing lasted long.

It was not so much a breakdown in communication as a gap in her concentration. She was always surprised how impatient they were. Through their clothes she heard a constant, pulsing whisper: IS IT? *IS IT YOU?*

It was never her: one invite to the pictures, one night at a dance, *a* kiss goodbye.

They could not wait to be *certain*.

Pub by the canal: black water, hairy reeds. Weeds bloomed underwater. A runner pounded, head back, weighted ankles. Clouds of ash. Nice arms, *great* legs. She always appreciated beauty – Crispin, Charley, Harley, Roge – an eyebrow, the line of a chin.

Roge came with the pints of bitter, a crisp packet in his

mouth. They sat on his coat sipping. Daylight shrank around them. She forgot to say anything. Petroleum sunset. Roge began to cry. Sometimes they cried. 'Never mind,' she said. She patted his ankle, totally understanding. 'We'll just have our drinks, eh.' She was always helpful at endings: her forté.

'It must be you,' her mother said, deadheading. 'What happened to whatshisname?' Gary, Martin, Jim, Wayne. Then her mother ceased to ask. Years passed. Her mother ceased. The girls at the bank said, 'Seeing anyone?'

She answered: Yes. Harry, Barry, Georgie, Cash.

Dan, Don, Will, Zed. Though sometimes, something happened with time, place, face and name; they mixed up. Dirk? Jason, Timmy . . . God. Was it Malcolm? Simon? Kirk?

Simon drove her to a beach on a bank holiday. He was in a rage. He could not bear blackened avocado paste. He could not stand sand in his sandwiches. She watched the sea steal the beach. Simon screamed. He slammed a car door: 'I told you to LOCK that door.' She said, 'Simon, we're alone on a beach,' but she said this quietly because she knew, due to her former experiences.

Kelvin. John.

John. John. John.

Sometimes she said, 'Slow down.'

She said, as doors slammed, 'What's the rush?'

Peruvian faces at the Photographers Gallery with Zim. Then, cappuccino after cappuccino. He *knew* Peru. The peasants were extremely healthy-looking indeed: burst veins on their noses, scarlet, short blunt limbs . . . She looked at Zim: his eyes, nose, his moving mouth, the Adam's apple working like a bronze yo-yo. He said, 'Do stop me if I'm boring you.' He was very beautiful indeed. She couldn't think of what he wanted her to say. He shook her hand outside Exit, walked, very firmly, away.

Paul. Lots of them like Paul. They walked on the heath. Paul's children from a former liaison – his 'significant other' this, his 'significant other' that – ran on ahead. Little Josie and Bartok: batik jump suits, silver coins for hair. He swung her arm up, formed an apex; the children ran under them, squealing. He screamed, 'Aren't they great?' but she was miles away already. 'Mmm,' she said, only, and that was her mistake.

Her desk began to serve students, an Enterprise Culture Scheme. They became young:

Baz, Keith, Jack, younger younger young.

But she still heard, through their grunge, through their rags, under their tattoos: Is it? Is It You?

Jack played in a band, smashed the drums up at the back in a leatherette tank top. Wringing wet, his face in love. He'd splash his hands down in their hairy arm gloves, splash his lager top, her cheek right in there, in his deep arm pit. She liked his flowery-deodorant sweat. But, she didn't know anything about music or hunt sabotage, she couldn't pretend. And, he found out.

Bernard, James, Kevvy, Mack . . .

The list went on, and on and on: the same old thing, the same young thing, different day.

Alone in bed.

At first she slept with them but no one caught her drift. Then as years passed, she would, but they would not, unless they were *certain* because of the many diseases and time-wasting risks involved. And they were in a hurry to be certain. Is it, *is it you?* Always alone in bed. Yet, she was heroic and never grew bitter or stayed in. She accepted all, reasonable, invitations. Her plait turned silver. 'Seeing anyone?' Yes. Denny, Peter, Henry, Kane. She always went out.

She was always out.

TIME TO GO

EDDIE TOOK ME by the shoulders outside Zeeb's, giving me a shake, going, 'What d'you think then eh, time to, is it, time to go?' I thought he was going to jump me or fucking something, for a second, breathing at me. I said, 'I think you're off your face.' He says, 'Turn around *now* Tommy,' like Bob Monkhouse, or one of those game show hosts, then he turned me around and the BMW is lying under the lamppost, creamy, asking for it. He says 'You have won . . . '

We hijacked this BMW, wrapped it round London, stripped it of its assets then dumped it near Eddie's van, got in Eddie's van and belted into the country, going on two wheels, turning on a penny, like turning on a corner in the Grand Prix. That's Eddie, fast Eddie. Brillionto. I'm rolling in the back. I've got dust in my nose and I'm sneezing. I'm falling against something really fucking slimy in a plastic bag. It could be an old rug or an old man. It could be someone dead. Eddie's van's so fucking funny. What's in it and you can see out all over the place, all the corners held together, rusty-lacy like somebody fucking knitted it. You can see the sky. You can see the fucking moon through a hole in the roof. It's like, right, when we were kids Eddie let me go, he let me go down a hill, in my pram, except it's so fucking noisy, back-firing and shuddering and now, it's shooting! I try to tell Eddie this, that we're driving in my pram, but it's so fucking funny I can't. Eddie's thinking. He's thinking and smoking. When he's thinking it's like he's got a pain, he's got these sore-looking lips, his face is screwed right up against the windscreen because he's got no lights. He had some but he smashed them up in a fight. Rammed this smarm who beeped him, this bloke in a Jag. Eddie shot after him like a fucking bullet, flew over a roundabout, rammed him. This bloke's face – lost his arse.

I'm laughing, I'm singing, 'We're all going for a – fucking holiday . . . '

We're in there hours down, up, round, up motorways but the miles go under us like it's minutes and Eddie's listing all the things he's done they know about and all the things he done they don't. He says, 'Tommy, Tommy, they'll send me down, they'll put me away and all that Jimmy Cagney shit.' I say, 'They'll never catch us on this horse.'

Me and Eddie. Me and Eddie we go all the way back to school. We were bunking off then. My mum and his mum coming to get us, bringing us back, ready or not. Once we hid out in a wood for, right, about a week. Eddie built this house.

All the concrete stops then it's fields and trees and more trees. Then it's like – proper trees, like nothing you see in a park. Thick, tall, wide. Eddie drops from 100 m.p.h. to a dead 5. I say, 'Spooky, it's spooky.' Then it gets so dark we can't see nothing and I'm up front, with my arm out. I'm swinging a torch. I'm still singing. I'm making stripes. Then Eddie says, '*Don't mess* Tommy,' so I stop then as it's a bit serious. Like we could get seriously dead. A little lane. A tree tunnel. Not exactly a main road. Tracks. I say, 'This isn't England. Why, it's THE TWILIGHT ZONE nimmy-nimmy . . . ' The ground is smoking. It's black. Smoky, black. Then we've got to drive so slowly these electric eyes, fucking weird, rabbits and foxes and things, the country, squirrels or rats, we're practically on top of them and they just look up and stroll off. They stroll off all casual and then they rummage about in the trees like they've gone demented.

We're going somewhere Eddie knows, somewhere brillianto-mondo.

The music, the whole fucking thing, was doing my head in. We'd been to this gig at Zeeb's, Stamford Hill, and it was alright, and Zeeb looked gorgeous, as usual. She looks like the others, dusty black clothes, dry locks, but she don't. She's got this creamy skin for a start. This plummy mouth. She thinks she's really fucking luscious. She really rates herself. The thing about her is she smells fucking lovely, spicey; this oil she uses under her arms, in the hairs, it's weird. It's really – sexy. It hangs about in your head. I think she could patent it. But it was all, like so what? The music . . . the whole fucking thing. She don't do nothing for me. She thinks she does but she don't. She was Jake's. Over him like a spider. She gets them and then she does something to them. Like I'd seen Jake, outside, in a car park, sobbing, fucking shaking on a wall. Not exactly – hard. And the way he looks at her like he's been starved. Sometimes I think me and Eddie, we're the only hard ones left.

I'd been there . . . hours, all my life. I'd got more than the hump. Fined that morning, wiped out and someone did my room, my amp, my mattress . . . wrecked . . . my head. I'd been there hours. Fucked off. A million people dron-going up and down and all the dogs tied up and howling on the stairs. I was smoking on top of the fridge and Zeeb goes she wants to talk to me ALONE, fucking capital letters, meaning she wants Eddie. It's what I've known. Jake's out, Eddie's in. She wants Eddie. I thought, she wants Eddie. She wants Eddie crying on a wall. She gave this little tilt of her head so her earrings jangled, and her smell came for me, wanting me to middle-man like I'd done for her and Jake and a few before for a bit of gear, for a laugh, and I hadn't planned to, but I said no. She couldn't believe it. Her eyes smarted but I didn't feel nothing for her. I thought, she's one inch away from fucking vicious. She says, 'Why not, *you* want him . . . ?' I pushed into this room Zeeb painted pink as far as she could reach with the paint brush so it's jagged pink up to my nose and it's lime green after that. I'd thought it was funny before, but now I think it's really fucking pathetic she couldn't be bothered to fetch a chair to stand on or borrow a fucking ladder. I thought, I'm fucking sick of this and my fucking life. I fucking hate London. There was this crowd on the floor crunching on empty beer tins. Eddie was lying half on this girl. I could see his tongue in her ear. I said, 'Hallo, Eddie, who's the lovely lady?' He lifts himself straight up, grinning. Everything speeded up after that. That's the great thing about Eddie. When he's around everything's fast.

I'm driving with Eddie. I'm saying, Come on Eddie tell, where're we going. Is it a castle and he says no. Is it a caravan? No. Is it a tree house? No. Is it a fucking meadow, *another country* . . . ? We're crawling, inching it up this hill that's so steep it's like we're crawling like insects straight up a wall. We're going to topple off . . . It's not black out any more, we don't need the torch out any more, it's purple then navy, then a soft milky blue, but I keep swinging it. Then I have to get out and push the fucking van and Eddie up, pushing like I'm pushing up a boulder up above my head. The trees fall back like they've all fallen over so it's all – big. At the top Eddie gets out and we're leaning on the van, for a fag and to calm down my heart. It's going for my ribs. The hills are rolling around us. It's all gone lilac. It's sparkling like I'm crying, it's dew. I say, like a kid, 'Are . . . we . . . there . . . yet? Is this it?' I feel so – knackered. I feel so fucking happy. I bump Eddie's hip with mine. He does this funny thing; he holds my hand. He's blowing out smoke. After the smoke he says, 'Yeah.'

TOTAL JOY

I HEARD DOGS *roaring*, the sound, if you will imagine it, of Rotweillers stuck in a lift, or one Pit bull terrier stuck on a stick, and I would have been *in* terror, mortally afraid, except, you see, *I'd seen.*

There are fleas on me but there are no flies.

Can you not see the wires about the place and that small amplifier?

And let's take a trip to the lock up, round by the bins (the bins I frequent), draw the planks apart, fit your eye against that now. On the far wall, isn't that the black, oily outline of a fair-sized dog. Would you say they'd sprayed a dog? Would you say they'd sprayed a dog like you'd spray a beat-up car – with *paint*?

And would you ask yourself why?

Would you ask yourself why, now?

I'll tell about the Pig if you'll ask about the dog.

The night the Pig got his the moon was full and swollen; a milky, softly pulsing aureole; stars twinkling and blinking. A greenish gleam from the world. I was thinking if you looked up it wasn't so bad. If you kept on looking up you know it was sometimes fairly OK good. The Plough, the, something else like a Y. I was joining . . . the . . . dots.

Then, off for my dinner, back of the burger bar. Bins, tall metal drums – kit from a giant's reggae band – one fifty-five a.m. They set it off. Dogs. And, though I was expecting something *amplified* I leapt. And out leapt, out of a velvet-lined pit, this big black, onyx-lit beast, evil. I would have been in terror.

But I was not *in* terror for I knew.

I thought: keep your head, stay calm; that hound from hell is a mangy tan called Rex, Mikey, Ann . . . They've *sprayed it black*. They've slipped it something: LSD. Its jaw yapped out of sync with the sound. I stood stock still, a burger bap, like a pale stone, in my hand. The big black beasty sailed for my (especially padded) throat.

I heard their giggles: saw greasy teeth down the alley. Sniffed a familiar, foul, drift on the breeze.

Pig.

And flew, with my tonsil-waggle scream: *PIIIIIG.*

I was not asleep when he got it and so know exactly the time it was. On time I am an expert. For e.g., in winter I sleep for the one hour precisely in every twenty-four. In summer I like to have a little lie-in. In summer the life here is different. You get a different kind of a room mate. Now, for e.g., this summer has been long and it's upsetting because all the children leave home and take your friggy space and the longer the summer the more the friggy children come. Don't hurry me, son.

I was in my shop doorway, in disguise, quicker than you can say FLY. Black-out. Squares of light snapped out. The neighbourhood was playing All Possums Here Are Dead. I heard the Pig's white tank crunch along the street. I had my head down and reckon I'd made myself as much like a bit of stray debris as my considerable skills would allow. e.g., I was in a flattened cardboard box and my head was wrapped away in the *Mail* (*not* my preference). My heart had dropped, I heard it, plop right through me, plop plop, in a drain. All around and above I heard hearts hammer, pant, stop. I saw the Pig's white tank, the Pig and she, Misery, the ginger WPC, pull up outside the burger bar. It was two a.m. and not a minute before. I just know that. Take my word for it, throw it out, think why would I lie, why?

The Pig and Misery ran into the burger bar.

Imagine the hunt for invisible dogs!

Now, I'd had my turn earlier on. (When the Pig was away we did not play.) Once I'd spied the wire, that mean amplifier, I got my turn in quick. I'd been into the burger bar myself. The boys had been – preoccupied in that arctic kitchen glaze: square dancing on cockroaches, squirting sauce. I left them a biggish present in the bin. My autumnal collection. Now, it had taken me a fair while to collect. A variety of textures, a spectrum of woodland shades. As an extra thought I added my very own: formless, steaming, fresh. You learn to take your revenge. You know for why? You know what they do? You know what street solidarity is? They don't own the place and even if they did what would me taking a few leavings signify, what? I would be kind of recycling. I would be doing my best for that leaking layer of ozone. For the milky moon, stars . . . If I didn't eat it the rats would (and the rats here cruise about like cats). Now you'd think, for e.g., those boys in there would just put the left-overs in the bin in the back and think no more about it and so, therefore, my son, you would be considerably wrong. They take the left-overs: the cold, flabby, raggy, fried-forever eggs, burnt burgers, assorted frozen spheres, and throw them in the bin and then they *piss* all over the bin. I've seen five of those boy-bastards pissing, laughing. Their idea of *fun*. I said –

There's no point in hurrying me son, I do not respond. Not any more. I do not respond to violence.

I'm saying now . . . friggy . . . not . . . a –

Jameson's, son. Thanking you. Only the best.

Through my paper peephole I spied a blue-black beetle crawling on the paper bridge above my nose: the crack in its back, the obscene revelation of compressed, yellowish, humanish skin; a concertina of wings. The *stuff* crawling about on the earth. The dirt that tries to tap, scuttle into your mind. I shimmered out from under the doorway hood for relief, for a trip: an eye-widening moony glip at my bedroom roof; sky. The only way out is up.

No chance. Inside the electric square . . . Crash . . . Bang. One two three lavish splitter falls: the fruit-machines had gone. The Pig was mad: couldn't find the dogs. Imagine my rictus grin as I heard the boys from the bar get it one by one. I heard them slapped. The Pig whacked them with his Noise Spot Fines. I saw them hop, doubled up by the groin. I saw Misery turned away from the violence, faced away, miserably smoking a fag. It was two fifteen a.m. not a minute before, when the Pig and she came out of the burger bar. The Pig's pockets bulged, rattled with loot. Then, he grinned. I thought: stay calm. He broke it, wind: cracked toxic cheeks. Lifted his leg to accommodate his gas. I'd say I was fifteen feet away. The ginger Misery made one of those fin-like gestures with her hand, like she couldn't, could not bear any more. I'd seen her do that twenty dozen times before. Fifteen feet and I could still bloody smell it. Unzip him and imagine, if you will, the vulcanic poisons still gushing in his guts, entrails – yuck.

Do *not* go to the autopsy. The deceased, I'm telling you, was one boiled Pig bastard and a half.

We got it if we called him and we got it if we did not.

You know this Jameson's is lovely. This is a lovely drink. Now a lovely drink like this would become lovelier still with a bit of tobacco. Forty Marlboro and skins, a household box of matches and two packs of the Dutch rolling stuff. I imagine that would enhance . . . Thanking you.

I saw them get into the car and after one minute I closed my eyes and I was rocking myself towards dreamy dreamland when I heard his car door slam and heard the sound of him pissing himself out on the wall. And then I heard –

Now, I've been thinking, my feet will be very cold in winter, they will be for e.g., colder than a block of ice, so as I'll have the two blocks of ice . . . I'm thinking this now imagining the contrast between a whiskey heat in my belly, a whiskey heat in my lungs and my poor bloody feet which will be . . . Thanking you.

The darkness motes had turned, subtly, brown. A car purred along the road, its headlamps fog-dipped. I heard footsteps . . . running. No, I can't say if they were heavy or light, just foot-like footsteps. And, no, I don't know who dunnit. Someone dunnit who'd had it, had enough. Underneath the tank, I could see the Pig's blue-black boots and trouser legs, his piss turned golden, steaming and running in channels. Then I saw two feet in trainers standing next to him. I heard three shots, one after the other. Bang. Bang. Bang. I thought; he'll survive it. But, he did not.

That incredible, curious peace after violence. The death-ly quiet. It was like the sun had ignored natural law and come out during the night. It was like it was safe now to leave our nuclear bunkers and blink about in a new rubble-ised world. It was like (OK, imagine), miraculously surviv-ing a bloody car crash: wonder followed by uncontainable mirth. The WPC, ex-Misery. She will deny this, she will, but before she radioed in, before her (simulated) sobs, before she yelled all that great 'Oh My God, Officer, Officer Down,' she let us all go-go. She stepped, in slow-mo, out of the tank, a linger at the leaky Pig (his blood leaked like thick, grey cloth), she leaned on the bonnet, got her fags out and she – lit up. Squares of light snapped on. People emerged from rubbish, out of disguise, to gather by the tank. We all looked down. The boys from the bar rushed out, gaped. One of them rushed back in and set the dog track off. Baying Hounds from Hell. All feuds stilled. We all joined hands. All joined in for Ring-a-Ring-a-Pig. It lasted the length of her fag, not one second more not one second less: one whirling, burning minute.

Imagine – *total* joy.